C.1

398.2
SLE

Sleeping beauty &
other favourite
fairy tales

$12.45

DATE			
	205 T	DEC 14 '89	206
FEB 4 '90	105	JAN 10 '90	206
		JAN 16 '90	205
	105	JAN 24 '90	200
	203	MAR 6 '90	202
FEB 12 '92 MAR. 25	201		201
APR 26 '90	204		202 T
JUN 7 '96	205	MAY 11 '94	204
NOV 16 '90	206	FEB 7 '96	203
NOV 30 '90	206	MAY 16 '96	203
DEC 1 '90			
DEC 7 '90	206		

SLEEPING BEAUTY

AND OTHER FAVOURITE FAIRY TALES

SLEEPING BEAUTY
& OTHER FAVOURITE FAIRY TALES

CHOSEN AND TRANSLATED BY
ANGELA CARTER

ILLUSTRATED BY
MICHAEL FOREMAN

SCHOCKEN BOOKS · NEW YORK

First American edition published by Schocken Books 1984
10 9 8 7 6 5 4 3 2 1   84 85 86 87
Translation and original material © Angela Carter 1982
Illustrations © Michael Foreman 1982
Published by agreement with Victor Gollancz Ltd, London

Library of Congress Cataloging in Publication Data
Main entry under title:
Sleeping beauty & other favourite fairy tales.
    All the stories are by Charles Perrault except two
by Madame Le Prince de Beaumont.
    Contents: The sleeping beauty in the wood — Little
Red Riding Hood — Puss in boots — [etc.]
    1. Fairy tales—France. [1. Fairy tales. 2. Folk-
lore—France] I. Perrault, Charles, 1628–1703.
II. Le Prince de Beaumont, Madame (Marie), 1711–1780.
III. Carter, Angela, 1940–   . IV. Foreman, Michael,
1938–   ill. V. Title: Sleeping beauty and other
favourite fairy tales.
PZ8.S383   1984   398.2′1′0944   84–1451

Photoset in Great Britain by Rowland Phototypesetting Ltd,
Bury St Edmunds, Suffolk
Printed and bound in Italy by New Interlitho, Milan
ISBN 0-8052-3921-9

Contents

All the stories, except two, are by Charles Perrault. *Beauty and the Beast* and *Sweetheart* are by Madame Leprince de Beaumont.

SLEEPING BEAUTY

AND OTHER FAVOURITE FAIRY TALES

The Sleeping Beauty in the Wood

Once upon a time, there lived a king and a queen who were bitterly unhappy because they did not have any children. They visited all the clinics, all the specialists, made holy vows, went on pilgrimages and said their prayers regularly but with so little success that when, at long last, the queen finally *did* conceive and, in due course, gave birth to a daughter, they were both wild with joy. Obviously, this baby's christening must be the grandest of all possible christenings; for her godmothers, she would have as many fairies as they could find in the entire kingdom. According to the custom of those times, each fairy would make the child a magic present, so that the princess could acquire every possible perfection. After a long search, they managed to trace seven suitable fairies.

After the ceremony at the church, the guests went back to the royal palace for a party in honour of the fairy godmothers. Each of these important guests found her place was specially laid with a great dish of gold and a golden knife, fork and spoon studded with diamonds and rubies. But as the fairies took their seats, an uninvited guest came storming into the palace, deeply affronted because she had been forgotten—though

9

it was no wonder she'd been overlooked; this old fairy had hidden herself away in her tower for fifteen years and, since nobody had set eyes on her all that time, they thought she was dead, or had been bewitched. The king ordered a place to be laid for her at once but he could not give her a great gold dish and gold cutlery like the other fairies had because only seven sets had been made. The old fairy was very annoyed at that and muttered threats between her teeth. The fairy who sat beside her overheard her and suspected she planned to revenge herself by giving the little princess a very unpleasant present when the time for present giving came. She slipped away behind the tapestry so that she could have the last word, if necessary, and put right any harm the old witch might do the baby.

Now the fairies presented their gifts. The youngest fairy said the princess would grow up to be the loveliest woman in the world. The next said she would have the disposition of an angel, the third that she would be graceful as a gazelle, the fourth gave her the gift of dancing, the fifth of singing like a nightingale, and the sixth said she would be able to play any kind of musical instrument that she wanted to.

But when it came to the old fairy's turn, she shook with spite and announced that, in spite of her beauty and accomplishments, the princess was going to prick her finger with a spindle and die of it.

All the guests trembled and wept. But the youngest fairy stepped out from behind the tapestry and cried out:

"Don't despair, King and Queen; your daughter will not die—although, alas, I cannot undo entirely the magic of a senior-ranking fairy. The princess *will* prick her finger with a spindle but, instead of dying, she will fall into a deep sleep that will last for a hundred years. And at the end of a hundred years, the son of a king will come to wake her."

In spite of this comfort, the king did all he could to escape the curse; he forbade the use of a spindle, or even the possession of one, on pain of death, in all the lands he governed.

Fifteen or sixteen years went by. The king and queen were spending the summer at a castle in the country and one day the princess decided to explore, prowling through room after room until at last she climbed up a spiral staircase in a tower and came to an attic in which an old lady was sitting, along with her distaff, spinning, for this old lady had not heard how the king had banned the use of a spindle.

"Whatever are you doing, my good woman?" asked the princess.

"I'm spinning, my pretty dear," answered the old lady.

"Oh, how clever!" said the princess. "How do you do it? Give it to me so that I can see if I can do it, too!"

11

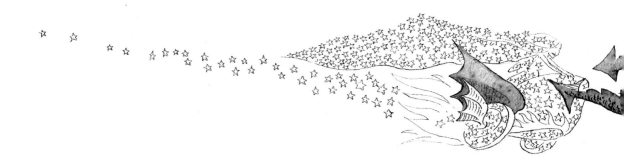

She was very lively and just a little careless; but besides, and most importantly, the fairies had ordained it. No sooner had she picked up the spindle than she pierced her hand with it and fell down in a faint.

The old lady cried for help and the servants came running from all directions. They threw water over her, unlaced her corsets, slapped her hands, rubbed her temples with eau-de-cologne—but nothing would wake her.

The king climbed to the attic to see the cause of the clamour and, sad at heart, knew the fairy's curse had come true. He knew the princess' time had come, just as the fairies said it would, and ordered her to be carried to the finest room in the palace and laid there on a bed covered with gold and silver embroidery. She was as beautiful as an angel. Her trance had not yet taken the colour from her face; her cheeks were rosy and her lips like coral. Her eyes were closed but you could hear her breathing very, very softly and, if you saw the slow movement of her breast, you knew she was not dead.

The king ordered she should be left in peace until the time came when she would wake up. At the moment the princess had pricked her finger, the good fairy who saved her life was in the realm of Mataquin, twelve thousand leagues away, but she heard the news immediately from a dwarf who sped to her in a pair of seven-league boots. The fairy left Mataquin at once in a fiery chariot drawn by dragons and arrived at the grieving court an hour later. The king went out to help her down; she approved of all his arrangements but she was very sensitive, and she thought how sad the princess would be when she woke up all alone in that great castle.

So she touched everything in the house, except for the king and queen, with her magic ring—the housekeepers, the maids of honour, the cham-

bermaids, the gentlemen-in-waiting, the court officials, the cooks, the scullions, the errand-boys, the night-watchmen, the Swiss guards, the page-boys, the footmen; she touched all the horses in the stable, and the stable-boys, too, and even Puff, the princess' little lap-dog, who was curled up on her bed beside her. As soon as she touched them with her magic ring, they all fell fast asleep and would not wake up until their mistress woke, ready to look after her when she needed them. Even the spits on the fire, loaded with partridges and pheasants, drowsed off to sleep, and the flames died down and slept, too. All this took only a moment; fairies are fast workers.

The king and queen kissed their darling child but she did not stir. Then they left the palace forever and issued proclamations forbidding anyone to approach it. Within a quarter of an hour, a great number of trees, some large, some small, interlaced with brambles and thorns, sprang up around the park and formed a hedge so thick that neither man nor beast could penetrate it. This hedge grew so tall that you could see only the topmost turrets of the castle, for the fairy had made a safe, magic place where the princess could sleep her sleep out free from prying eyes.

At the end of a hundred years, the son of the king who now ruled over the country went out hunting in that region. He asked the local people what those turrets he could see above the great wood might mean. They replied, each one, as he had heard tell—how it was an old ruin, full of ghosts; or, that all the witches of the country went there to hold their sabbaths. But the most popular story was, that it was the home of an ogre who carried all the children he caught there, to eat them at his leisure, knowing nobody else could follow him through the wood. The prince did not know what to believe. Then an old man said to him:

"My lord, fifty years ago I heard my father say that the most beautiful princess in all the world was sleeping in that castle, and her sleep was going to last for a hundred years, until the prince who is meant to have her comes to wake her up."

When he heard that, the young prince was tremendously excited; he had never heard of such a marvellous adventure and, fired with thoughts of love and glory, he made up his mind there and then to go through the wood. No sooner had he stepped among the trees than the great trunks and branches, the thorns and brambles parted, to let him pass. He saw the castle at the end of a great avenue and walked towards it, though he was surprised to see that none of his attendants could follow him because the trees sprang together again as soon as he had gone between them. But he did not abandon his quest. A young prince in love is always brave. Then he arrived at a courtyard that seemed like a place where only fear lived.

An awful silence filled it and the look of death was on everything. Man and beast stretched on the ground, like corpses; but the pimples on the red noses of the Swiss guards soon showed him they were not dead at all, but sleeping, and the glasses beside them, with the dregs of wine still at the bottoms, showed how they had dozed off after a spree.

He went through a marble courtyard; he climbed a staircase; he went into a guardroom, where the guards were lined up in two ranks, each with a gun on his shoulder, and snoring with all their might. He found several rooms full of gentlemen-in-waiting and fine ladies; some stood, some sat, all slept. At last he arrived in a room that was entirely covered in gilding and, there on a bed with the curtains drawn back so that he could see her clearly, lay a princess about fifteen or sixteen years old and she was so lovely that she seemed, almost, to shine. The prince approached her trembling, and fell on his knees before her.

The enchantment was over; the princess woke. She gazed at him so tenderly you would not have thought it was the first time she had ever seen him.

"Is it you, my prince?" she said. "You have kept me waiting for a long time."

The prince was beside himself with joy when he heard that and the tenderness in her voice overwhelmed him so that he hardly knew how to

reply. He told her he loved her better than he loved himself and though he stumbled over the words, that made her very happy, because he showed so much feeling. He was more tongue-tied than she, because she had had plenty of time to dream of what she would say to him; her good fairy had made sure she had sweet dreams during her long sleep. They talked for hours and still had not said half the things they wanted to say to one another.

But the entire palace had woken up with the princess and everyone was going about his business again. Since none of them were in love, they were all dying of hunger. The chief lady-in-waiting, just as ravenous as the rest, lost patience after a while and told the princess loud and clear that dinner was ready. The prince helped the princess up from the bed and she dressed herself with the greatest magnificence; but when she put on her ruff, the prince remembered how his grandmother had worn one just like it. All the princess' clothes were a hundred years out of fashion, but she was no less beautiful because of that.

Supper was served in the hall of mirrors, while the court orchestra played old tunes on violins and oboes they had not touched for a hundred years. After supper, the chaplain married them in the castle chapel and the chief lady-in-waiting drew the curtains round their bed for them. They did not sleep much, that night; the princess did not feel in the least drowsy. The prince left her in the morning, to return to his father's palace.

The king was anxious because his son had been away so long. The prince told him that he had lost himself in the forest while he was out hunting and had spent the night in a charcoal burner's hut, where his host had given him black bread and cheese to eat. The king believed the story but the queen, the prince's mother, was not so easily hoodwinked when she saw that now the young man spent most of his time out hunting in the forest. Though he always arrived back with an excellent excuse when he had spent two or three nights away from home, his mother soon guessed he was in love.

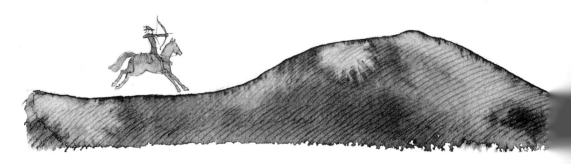

He lived with the princess for more than two years and he gave her two children. They named the eldest, a daughter, Dawn, because she was so beautiful but they called their son Day because he came after Dawn and was even more beautiful still.

The queen tried to persuade her son to tell her his secret but he dared not confide in her. Although he loved her, he feared her, because she came from a family of ogres and his father had married her only because she was very, very rich. The court whispered that the queen still had ogrish tastes and could hardly keep her hands off little children, so the prince thought it best to say nothing about his own babies.

But when the king died and the prince himself became king, he felt confident enough to publicly announce his marriage and install the new queen, his wife, in his royal palace with a great deal of ceremony. And soon after that, the new king decided to declare war on his neighbour, the Emperor Cantalabutte.

He left the governing of his kingdom in his mother's hands and he trusted her to look after his wife and children for him, too, because he would be away at war for the whole summer.

As soon as he was gone, the queen mother sent her daughter-in-law and her grandchildren away to the country, to a house deep in the woods, so that she could satisfy her hideous appetites with the greatest of ease. She herself arrived at the house a few days later and said to the butler:

"I want to eat little Dawn for my dinner tomorrow."

"Oh, my lady!" exclaimed the butler.

"She's just the very thing I fancy," said the queen mother in the voice of an ogress famished for fresh meat. "And I want you to serve her up with sauce Robert."

The poor man saw he could not argue with a hungry ogress, picked up a carving knife and went to little Dawn's room. She was just four years old. When she saw her dear friend, the butler, she ran up to him, laughing, threw her arms around his neck and asked him where her sweeties were. He

burst into tears and the knife fell from his hands. He went down to the farmyard and slaughtered a little lamb instead. He served the lamb up in such a delicious sauce the queen mother said she had never eaten so well in her life and he spirited little Dawn away from harm; he handed her over to his wife, who hid her in a cellar, in the servants' quarters.

Eight days passed. Then the ogress said to the butler:

"I want to eat little Day for my supper."

The butler was determined to outwit her again. He found little Day playing at fencing with his pet monkey; the child was only three. He took him to his wife, who hid him away with his sister, and served up a tender young kid in his place. The queen mother smacked her lips over the dish, so all went well until the night the wicked ogress said to the butler:

"I want to eat the queen with the same sauce you made for her children."

This time, the poor butler did not know what to do. The queen was twenty, now, if you did not count the hundred years she had been asleep; her skin was white and lovely but it was a little tough, and where in all the farmyard was he to find a beast with skin just like it? There was nothing for it; he must kill the queen to save himself and he went to her room, determined he would not have to enter it a second time. He rushed in with a dagger in his hand and told her her mother-in-law had ordered her to die.

"Be quick about it," she said calmly. "Do as she told you. When I am dead, I shall be with my poor children again, my children whom I love so much."

Because they had been taken away from her without a word of explanation, she thought they were dead.

The butler's heart melted.

"No, no, my lady, you don't need to die so that you can be with your children. I've hidden them away from the queen mother's hunger and I will trick her again, I will give her a young deer for supper instead of you."

He took her to the cellar, where he left her kissing her children and weeping over them, and went to kill a young doe that the queen mother ate for supper with as much relish as if it had been her daughter-in-law. She was very pleased with her own cruelty and practised telling her son how the wolves had eaten his wife and children while he had been away at the wars.

One night as she prowled about as usual, sniffing for the spoor of fresh

meat, she heard a voice coming from the servants' quarters. It was little Day's voice; he was crying because he had been naughty and his mother wanted to whip him. Then the queen mother heard Dawn begging her mother to forgive the little boy. The ogress recognised the voices of her grandchildren and she was furious. She ordered a huge vat to be brought into the middle of the courtyard. She had the vat filled with toads, vipers, snakes and serpents and then the queen, her children, the butler, his wife and his maid were brought in front of her with their hands tied behind their backs. She was going to have them thrown into the vat.

The executioners were just on the point of carrying out their dreadful instructions when the king galloped into the courtyard. Nobody had expected him back so soon. He was astonished at what he saw and asked who had commanded the vat and the bonds. The ogress was so angry to see her plans go awry that she jumped head-first into the vat and the vile beasts inside devoured her in an instant. The king could not help grieving a little; after all, she was his mother. But his beautiful wife and children soon made him happy again.

Moral

A brave, rich, handsome husband is a prize well worth waiting for; but no modern woman would think it was worth waiting for a hundred years. The tale of the Sleeping Beauty shows how long engagements make for happy marriages, but young girls these days want so much to be married I do not have the heart to press the moral.

Little Red Riding Hood

Once upon a time, deep in the heart of the country, there lived a pretty little girl whose mother adored her, and her grandmother adored her even more. This good woman made her a red hood like the ones that fine ladies wear when they go riding. The hood suited the child so much that soon everybody was calling her Little Red Riding Hood.

One day, her mother baked some cakes on the griddle and said to Little Red Riding Hood:

"Your granny is sick; you must go and visit her. Take her one of these cakes and a little pot of butter."

Little Red Riding Hood went off to the next village to visit her grandmother. As she walked through the wood, she met a wolf, who wanted to eat her but did not dare to because there were woodcutters working nearby. He asked her where she was going. The poor child did not know how dangerous it is to chatter away to wolves and replied innocently:

"I'm going to visit my grandmother to take her this cake and this little pot of butter from my mother."

"Does your grandmother live far away?" asked the wolf

"Oh yes," said Little Red Riding Hood. "She lives beyond the mill you can see over there, in the first house you come to in the village."

"Well, I shall go and visit her, too," said the wolf. "I will take *this* road and you shall take *that* road and let's see who can get there first."

The wolf ran off by the shortest path and Red Riding Hood went off the longest way and she made it still longer because she dawdled along, gathering nuts and chasing butterflies and picking bunches of wayside flowers.

The wolf soon arrived at Grandmother's house. He knocked on the door, rat tat tat.

"Who's there?"

"Your grand-daughter, Little Red Riding Hood," said the wolf, disguising his voice. "I've brought you a cake baked on the griddle and a little pot of butter from my mother."

Grandmother was lying in bed because she was poorly. She called out:
"Lift up the latch and walk in!"

The wolf lifted the latch and opened the door. He had not eaten for three days. He threw himself on the good woman and gobbled her up. Then he closed the door behind him and lay down in Grandmother's bed to wait for Little Red Riding Hood. At last she came knocking on the door, rat tat tat.

"Who's there?"

Little Red Riding Hood heard the hoarse voice of the wolf and thought that her grandmother must have caught a cold. She answered:

"It's your grand-daughter, Little Red Riding Hood. I've brought you a cake baked on the griddle and a little pot of butter from my mother."

The wolf disguised his voice and said:

"Lift up the latch and walk in."

Little Red Riding Hood lifted the latch and opened the door.

When the wolf saw her come in, he hid himself under the bedclothes and said to her:

"Put the cake and the butter down on the bread-bin and come and lie down with me."

Little Red Riding Hood took off her clothes and went to lie down in the bed. She was surprised to see how odd her grandmother looked. She said to her:

"Grandmother, what big arms you have!"

"All the better to hold you with, my dear."

"Grandmother, what big legs you have!"

"All the better to run with, my dear."

"Grandmother, what big ears you have!"

"All the better to hear with, my dear."

"Grandmother, what big eyes you have!"

"All the better to see with, my dear!"

"Grandmother, what big teeth you have!"

"All the better to eat you up!"

At that, the wicked wolf threw himself upon Little Red Riding Hood and gobbled her up, too.

Moral

Children, especially pretty, nicely brought-up young ladies, ought never to talk to strangers; if they are foolish enough to do so, they should not be surprised if some greedy wolf consumes them, elegant red riding hoods and all.

Now, there are real wolves, with hairy pelts and enormous teeth; but also wolves who seem perfectly charming, sweet-natured and obliging, who pursue young girls in the street and pay them the most flattering attentions.

Unfortunately, these smooth-tongued, smooth-pelted wolves are the most dangerous beasts of all.

Puss in Boots

A certain poor miller had only his mill, his ass and his cat to bequeath to his three sons when he died. The children shared out their patrimony and did not bother to call in the lawyers; if they had done so, they would have been stripped quite bare of course. The eldest took the mill, the second the ass and the youngest had to make do with the cat.

He felt himself very ill used.

"My brothers can earn an honest living with their inheritance, but once I've eaten my cat and made a muff with his pelt, I shall have to die of hunger."

The cat overheard him but decided to pretend he had not done so; he addressed his master gravely.

"Master, don't fret; give me a bag and a pair of boots to protect my little feet from the thorny undergrowth and you'll see that your father hasn't provided for you so badly, after all."

Although the cat's master could not really believe his cat would support him, he had seen him play so many cunning tricks when he went to catch rats and mice—he would hang upside down by his feet; or hide himself in the meal and play at being dead—that he felt a faint hope his cat might think up some helpful scheme.

When the cat had got what he asked for, he put on his handsome boots and slung the bag round his neck, keeping hold of the draw-strings with his two front paws. He went to a warren where he knew there were a great many rabbits. He put some bran and a selection of juicy weeds at the bottom of the bag and then stretched out quite still, like a corpse, and waited for some ingenuous young rabbit to come and investigate the bag and its appetising contents.

No sooner had he lain down than a silly bunny jumped into the bag. Instantly, the cat pulled the draw-strings tight and killed the rabbit without mercy.

Proudly bearing his prey, he went to the king and asked to speak to him. He was taken to his majesty's private apartment. As soon as he got inside the door, he made the king a tremendous bow and said:

"Sire, may I present you with a delicious young rabbit that my master, the Marquis of Carabas, ordered me to offer you, with his humblest compliments."

Without his master's knowledge or consent, the cat had decided the miller's son should adopt the name of the Marquis of Carabas.

"Tell your master that I thank him with all my heart," said the king.

The next day, the cat hid himself in a cornfield, with his open bag, and two partridges flew into it. He pulled the strings and caught them both. Then he went to present them to the king, just as he had done with the rabbit. The king accepted the partridges with great glee and rewarded the cat with a handsome tip.

The cat kept on taking his master's game to the king for two or three months. One day, he learned that the king planned to take a drive along the riverside with his beautiful daughter. He said to his master:

"If you take my advice, your fortune is made. You just go for a swim in the river at a spot I'll show to you and leave the rest to me."

The Marquis of Carabas obediently went off to swim, although he could not think why the cat should want him to. While he was bathing, the king drove by and the cat cried out with all its might:

"Help! Help! The Marquis of Carabas is drowning!"

The king put his head out of his carriage window when he heard this commotion and recognised the cat who had brought him so much game.

He ordered his servants to hurry and save the Marquis of Carabas.

While they were pulling the marquis out of the river, the cat went to the king's carriage and told him how robbers had stolen his master's clothes while he swam in the river even though he'd shouted "Stop thief!" at the top of his voice. In fact, the cunning cat had hidden the miller's son's wretched clothes under a stone.

The king ordered the master of his wardrobe to hurry back to the palace and bring a selection of his own finest garments for the Marquis of Carabas to wear. When the young man put them on, he looked very handsome and the king's daughter thought: "What an attractive young man!" The Marquis of Carabas treated her with respect mingled with tenderness and she fell madly in love.

The king invited the Marquis of Carabas to join him in his carriage and continue the drive in style. The cat was delighted to see his scheme begin to succeed and busily ran ahead of the procession. He came to a band of peasants who were mowing a meadow and said:

"Good people, if you don't tell the king that this meadow belongs to the Marquis of Carabas, I'll make mincemeat of every one of you."

As soon as he saw the mowers, the king asked them who owned the hayfield. They had been so intimidated by the cat that they dutifully chorused:

"It belongs to the Marquis of Carabas."

"You have a fine estate," remarked the king to the marquis.

"The field crops abundantly every year," improvised the marquis.

The cat was still racing ahead of the party and came to a band of harvesters. He said to them:

"Good harvesters, if you don't say that all these cornfields belong to the Marquis of Carabas, I'll make mincemeat of every one of you."

The king passed by a little later and wanted to know who owned the rolling cornfield.

"The Marquis of Carabas possesses them all," said the harvesters.

The king expressed his increasing admiration of the marquis' estates. The cat ran before the carriage and made the same threats to everyone he met on the way; the king was perfectly astonished at the young man's great possessions.

At last the cat arrived at a castle. In this castle, lived an ogre. This ogre was extraordinarily rich; he was the true owner of all the land through which the king had travelled. The cat had taken good care to find out all he could about this ogre and now he asked the servant who answered the door if he could speak to him; he said he couldn't pass so close by the castle without paying his respects to such an important man as its owner.

The ogre made him as welcome as an ogre can.

"I'm told you can transform yourself into all sorts of animals," said the cat. "That you can change yourself into a lion, for example; or even an elephant."

"Quite right," replied the ogre. "Just to show you, I'll turn myself into a lion."

When he found himself face to face with a lion, even our cat was so scared that he jumped up on to the roof and balanced there precariously because his boots weren't made for walking on tiles.

As soon as the ogre had become himself again, the cat clambered down and confessed how terrified he had been.

"But gossip also has it—though I can scarcely believe it—that you also have the power to take the shapes of the very smallest animals. They say you can even shrink down as small as a rat, or a mouse. But I must admit, even if it seems rude, that I think that's quite impossible."

"Impossible?" said the ogre. "Just you see!" He changed into a mouse and began to scamper around on the floor. The cat no sooner saw him than he jumped on him and gobbled him up.

Meanwhile, the king saw the ogre's fine castle as he drove by and decided to pay it a visit. The cat heard the sound of carriage wheels on the drawbridge, ran outside and greeted the king.

"Welcome, your majesty, to the castle of the Marquis of Carabas."

"What sir? Does this fine castle also belong to you? I've never seen anything more splendid than this courtyard and the battlements that surround it; may we be permitted to view the interior?"

The marquis gave his hand to the young princess and followed the king. They entered a grand room where they found a banquet ready prepared; the ogre had invited all his friends to a dinner party, but none of the guests dared enter the castle when they saw the king had arrived. The king was delighted with the good qualities of the Marquis of Carabas and his daughter was beside herself about them. There was also the young man's immense wealth to be taken into account. After his fifth or sixth glass of wine, the king said:

"Say the word, my fine fellow, and you shall become my son-in-law."

The marquis bowed very low, immediately accepted the honour the king bestowed on him and married the princess that very day. The cat was made a great lord and gave up hunting mice, except for pleasure.

Moral

A great inheritance may be a fine thing; but hard work and ingenuity will take a young man further than his father's money

Another moral

If a miller's son can so quickly win the heart of a princess, that is because clothes, bearing and youth speedily inspire affection; and the means to achieve them are not always entirely commendable.

Bluebeard

There once lived a man who owned fine town houses and fine country houses, dinner services of gold and silver, tapestry chairs and gilded coaches; but, alas, God had also given him a blue beard, which made him look so ghastly that women fled at the sight of him.

A certain neighbour of his was the mother of two beautiful daughters. He decided to marry one or other of them, but he left the girls to decide between themselves which of them should become his wife; whoever would take him could have him. But neither of them wanted him; both felt a profound distaste for a man with a blue beard. They were even more suspicious of him because he had been married several times before and nobody knew what had become of his wives.

In order to make friends with the girls, Bluebeard threw a lavish house-party at one of his country mansions for the sisters, their mother, three or four of their closest friends and several neighbours. The party lasted for eight whole days. Every day there were elaborate parties of pleasure—fishing, hunting, dancing, games, feasting. The guests hardly slept at all but spent the night playing practical jokes on one another.

Everything went so well that the youngest daughter began to think that the beard of the master of the house was not so very blue, after all; that he was, all in all, a very fine fellow.

As soon as they returned to town, the marriage took place.

After a month had passed, Bluebeard told his wife he must leave her to her own devices for six weeks or so; he had urgent business in the provinces and must attend to it immediately. But he urged her to enjoy herself while he was away; her friends should visit her and, if she wished, she could take them to the country with her. But, above all, she must keep in good spirits.

"Look!" he said to her. "Here are the keys of my two large attics, where the furniture is stored; this is the key to the cabinet in which I keep the dinner services of gold and silver that are too good to use every day; these are the keys of the strong-boxes in which I keep my money; these are the keys of my chests of precious stones; and this is the pass key that will let you into every one of the rooms in my mansion. Use these keys freely. All is yours. But this little key, here, is the key of the room at the end of the long gallery on the ground floor; open everything, go everywhere, but I absolutely forbid you to go into that little room and, if you so much as open the door, I warn you that nothing will spare you from my wrath."

She promised to do as he told her. He kissed her, got into his carriage and drove away.

Her friends and neighbours did not wait until she sent for them to visit her. They were all eager to see the splendours of her house. None of them had dared to call while the master was at home because his blue beard was so offensive. But now they could explore all the rooms at leisure and each one was more sumptuous than the last. They climbed into the attics and were lost for words with which to admire the number and beauty of the tapestries, the beds, the sofas, the cabinets, the tables, and the long mirrors, some of which had frames of glass, others of silver or gilded vermilion—all more magnificent than anything they had ever seen. They never stopped congratulating their friend on her good luck, but she took no pleasure from the sight of all this luxury because she was utterly consumed with the desire to open the door of the forbidden room.

Her curiosity so tormented her that, at last, without stopping to think how rude it was to leave her friends, she ran down the little staircase so fast she almost tripped and broke her neck. When she reached the door of the forbidden room, she stopped for a moment and remembered that her husband had absolutely forbidden her to go inside. She wondered if he would punish her for being disobedient; but the temptation was so strong she could not resist it. She took the little key, and, trembling, opened the door.

The windows were shuttered and at first she could see nothing; but, after a few moments, her eyes grew accustomed to the gloom and she saw that the floor was covered with clotted blood. In the blood lay the corpses of all the women whom Bluebeard had married and then murdered, one after the other. She thought she was going to die of fright and the key fell from her hand. After she came to her senses, she picked up the key, closed the door and climbed back to her room to recover herself.

She saw the key of this forbidden room was stained with blood and washed it. But the blood would not go away, so she washed it again. Still the blood-stain stayed. She washed it, yet again, more carefully, then scrubbed it with soap and sandstone; but the blood-stain would not budge. It was a magic key and nothing could clean it. When the blood was scrubbed from one side of the key, the stain immediately reappeared on the other side.

That same night, Bluebeard returned unexpectedly from his journey; a letter had arrived on the way to tell him that his business had already been satisfactorily settled in his absence. His wife did all she could to show him how delighted she was to have him back with her so quickly.

Next day, he asked her for his keys; she gave them to him but her hand was trembling so badly he guessed what had happened.

"How is it that the key of the little room is no longer with the others?" he asked.

"I must have left it upstairs on my dressing-table," she said, flustered.

"Give it to me," said Bluebeard.

She made excuse after excuse but there was no way out; she must go and fetch the key. Bluebeard examined it carefully and said to his wife:

"Why is there blood on this key?"

"I don't know," quavered the poor woman, paler than death.

"You don't know!" said Bluebeard. "But *I* know, very well! You have opened the door of the forbidden room. Well, madame, now you have opened it, you may step straight inside it and take your place beside the ladies whom you have seen there!"

She threw herself at her husband's feet, weeping and begging his forgiveness; she was truly sorry she had been disobedient. She was so beautiful and so distressed that the sight of her would have melted a heart of stone, but Bluebeard's heart was harder than any stone.

"You must die, madame," he said. "And you must die quickly."

She looked at him with eyes full of tears and pleaded:

"Since I must die, give me a little time to pray."

Bluebeard said: "I'll give you a quarter of an hour, but not one moment more."

As soon as she was alone, she called to her sister, Anne, and said:

"Sister Anne, climb to the top of the tower and see if my brothers are coming; they told me they would come to visit me today and if you see them, signal to them to hurry."

Sister Anne climbed to the top of the tower and the poor girl called out to her every minute or so:

"Sister Anne, Sister Anne, do you see anybody coming?"

And Anne, her sister, would reply:

"I see nothing but the sun shining and the grass growing green."

Bluebeard took an enormous cutlass in his hand and shouted to his wife: "Come down at once, or I'll climb up to you!"

"Oh, please, I beg you—just a moment more!" she implored, and called out, in a lower voice: "Sister Anne, Sister Anne, do you see anybody coming?"

Sister Anne replied:

"I see nothing but the sun shining and the grass growing green."

"Come down at once, or I'll climb up to you!" cried Bluebeard.

"I'll be down directly," his wife assured him; but still she whispered: "Sister Anne, Sister Anne, do you see anything coming?"

"I see a great cloud of dust drawing near from the edge of the horizon."

"Is it the dust my brothers make as they ride towards me?"

"Oh, no—it is the dust raised by a flock of sheep!"

"Will you never come down?" thundered Bluebeard.

"Just one moment more!" begged his wife and once again she demanded: "Sister Anne, Sister Anne, do you see anything coming?"

"I see two horsemen in the distance, still far away. Thank God!" she cried a moment later. "They are our brothers; I shall signal to them to hurry."

Bluebeard now shouted so loudly that all the house trembled. His unfortunate wife went down to him and threw herself in tears at his feet, her dishevelled hair tumbling all around her.

"Nothing you can do will save you," said Bluebeard. "You must die." With one hand, he seized her disordered hair and, with the other, raised his cutlass in the air; he meant to chop off her head with it. The poor woman turned her terrified eyes upon him and begged him for a last moment in which to prepare for death.

"No, no!" he said. "Think of your maker." And so he lifted up his cutlass. At that moment came such a loud banging on the door that Bluebeard stopped short. The door opened and in rushed two horsemen with naked blades in their hands.

He recognised his wife's two brothers; one was a dragoon, the other a

musketeer. He fled, to save himself, but the two brothers trapped him before he reached the staircase. They thrust their swords through him and left him for dead. Bluebeard's wife was almost as overcome as her husband and did not have enough strength left to get to her feet and kiss her brothers.

Bluebeard left no heirs, so his wife took possession of all his estate. She used part of it to marry her sister Anne to a young man with whom she had been in love for a long time; she used more of it to buy commissions for her two brothers; and she used the rest to marry herself to an honest man who made her forget her sorrows as the wife of Bluebeard.

Moral

Curiosity is a charming passion but may only be satisfied at the price of a thousand regrets; one sees around one a thousand examples of this sad truth every day. Curiosity is the most fleeting of pleasures; the moment it is satisfied, it ceases to exist and it always proves very, very expensive.

Another moral

It is easy to see that the events described in this story took place many years ago. No modern husband would dare to be half so terrible, nor to demand of his wife such an impossible thing as to stifle her curiosity. Be he never so quarrelsome or jealous, he'll toe the line as soon as she tells him to. And whatever colour his beard might be, it's easy to see which of the two is the master.

The Foolish Wishes

There once lived a woodcutter who was so poor he couldn't enjoy life at all; he thought he was by nature a most unlucky fellow.

One day, at work in the woods, he was moaning away, as usual, when Jupiter, king of the gods, appeared unexpectedly, thunderbolt in hand. The woodcutter was very frightened and threw himself on the ground, apologising profusely for ever having complained about anything at all.

"Don't be scared," said Jupiter. "I'm deeply touched by your misfortunes. Listen. I am the king of the gods and the master of the world. I'm going to grant you three wishes. Anything you want, anything at all, whatever will make you happy—all you have to do is wish for it. But think very carefully befor you make your wishes, because they're the only ones you'll ever get."

At that, Jupiter went noisily back to heaven and the woodcutter picked up his bundle of sticks and trudged home, light at heart. "I mustn't wish for anything silly," he said to himself. "Must talk it over with the wife before I make a decision."

When he reached his cottage, he told his wife, Fanchon, to pile more wood on the fire.

"We're going to be rich!" he said. "All we've got to do is to make three wishes."

He told her what had happened to him and she was dazzled at the prospects that opened up before her. But she thought they should plan their wishes very carefully.

"Blaise, my dear, don't let's spoil everything by being too hasty. Let's talk things over, and put off making our first wish until tomorrow, after we've had a good night's sleep."

"Quite right," said Blaise, her husband. "But let's celebrate; let's have a glass of wine."

She drew some wine from the barrel and he rested his bones in his armchair beside a roaring fire, glass in hand, happier than he had ever been in his life.

"My, oh, my," he said, half to himself. "I know just what would go down well on a night like this; a nice piece of black pudding. Why, I wish I had a piece of black pudding right now!"

No sooner had he spoken these fateful words than Fanchon beheld an enormous black pudding make an unexpected appearance in the chimney corner and come crawling towards her like a snake. First, she screamed; then, when she realised that the black pudding had arrived solely because her stupid husband had made a careless wish, she called him every name under the sun and heaped abuse on his head.

"We could have had an entire empire of our own! Gold and pearls and diamonds and nice clothes, any amount of them—and what do you go and wish for? What's your heart's desire—why, a bit of black pudding!"

"Well, I'm sorry," he said, "What else can I say— I admit it, I've done something very foolish. I'll do better, next time. Haven't I said I'm sorry?"

"Words, words, words," said the woodcutter's wife. "Why don't you go and sleep in the stable; it's the best place for an ass like you."

Her husband lost his temper completely at that and thought how much he'd like to wish to be a widower; but he didn't quite dare say it aloud.

"Men were born to suffer! To hell with the black pudding! I wish that black pudding were hanging from the end of your nose!"

Now, Fanchon was a very pretty woman and nobody would have said her looks were improved by the black pudding but it hung over her mouth and muffled her nagging and, for a single, happy moment, her husband felt he could wish for nothing more.

"After these disasters," he announced, "we must be more prudent. I think I shall use my last remaining wish to make myself a king."

But, all the same, he had to take the queen's feelings into account; how would she like to be a queen and sit on a throne when she had a nose as long as a donkey's? And, because only one wish was left, that was the choice before them—either King Blaise had for his consort the ugliest queen in the world; or they used the wish to get rid of the pudding and Blaise the woodcutter had his pretty wife again.

Fanchon, however, thought there was no choice at all. She wanted her nose in its original condition. Nothing more.

So the woodcutter stayed in his cottage and went out to saw logs every day. He did not become a king; he did not even fill his pockets with money. He was only too glad to use the last wish to make things as they had been again.

Moral

Greedy, short-sighted, careless, thoughtless, changeable people don't know how to make sensible decisions; and few of us are capable of using well the gifts God gave us, anyway.

Beauty and the Beast

Once upon a time, there lived a rich merchant who gave his three sons and his three daughters the best that money could buy. They had private tutors for everything. All the girls were very pretty, especially the youngest. When she was a baby, she was nick-named "Little Beauty", and the name stayed with her as she grew older, which did not please her sisters much. This youngest sister was not only the best looking but also a much nicer person than the others, who were stuck-up because they were so rich, and snobs, too. They liked to mingle with the high and mighty and all their pleasures were expensive ones—dancing at the grandest balls; the front stalls at the theatre; going walking in the park wearing the most beautiful clothes. They made fun of the youngest because she preferred to stay at home with a good book.

Because they were so wealthy, successful businessmen often wanted to marry them, but the two eldest said they would never marry—no! not until they found a duke, or a count. Beauty, the youngest, thanked everyone politely for their proposals but said she was too young to marry yet, and wanted to stay with her father a little while longer.

Then, quite suddenly, the merchant lost everything. No money was left. All he possessed now was a little house far away in the country. He could not help but cry when he told his sophisticated children they must go there to till the soil with their own hands to scratch a living, and the two elder girls announced that, since they did not wish to leave town, they would avail themselves of some of those proposals of marriage. But now they were no longer heiresses, their former suitors would not even look at them.

All the enemies those girls had made with their arrogant ways said: "Don't waste your pity on those two! Pride goes before a fall. Let them see how long they can keep up their high-faluting ways among the sheep and chickens." But, at the same time, everybody said: "Poor Beauty, how sorry we are for her. She never thought she was too good for ordinary folks. She was so gentle and so generous."

The men who wanted to marry her when she was rich redoubled their efforts to do so now she had nothing. But she told them she could not possibly abandon her father in his misfortune, and must go with him to the country, to console him and to toil beside him. At first she fretted to lose all the good things money had bought her, but then she told herself to pull herself together: "I can cry as much as I like, but it won't do me any good. I shall try to be happy without a penny."

When they arrived at their new home, the merchant and his three sons set to work on the land, while Beauty got up at four in the morning, cleaned the house and got their dinners ready. At first, she tired herself out because she was not used to rough work but after a month or so she grew stronger, and her health was never better. Once her housework was finished, she would read, or play the harpsichord, or sing at the spinning wheel. Her two sisters, quite the contrary, were bored to death. They dragged themselves out of bed at noon and spent their days in useless pottering, lamenting the loss of their lovely clothes and grand friends.

"Look at our sister!" they said to one another. "You can see she always had the temperament of a housemaid. She's perfectly happy doing the chores."

The merchant did not agree with them. He knew his Beauty hid her light under a bushel for his sake, loved her all the more, and respected her too, because her lazy sisters not only left every scrap of housework to her, but then teased and abused her all day long.

The family lived like this for an entire year, until the merchant received a letter telling him how a ship that carried goods of his, a ship he feared was lost, had arrived at last safe in port. The news turned the heads of the eldest girls straightaway and they eagerly clamoured for presents. Their father must bring them back new dresses, new jewellery, new hats, all sorts of gewgaws. But Beauty asked for nothing, because she was sure her father would never be able to sell his cargo for sufficient money to pay for half the things her sisters wanted.

"You haven't asked me to bring you anything, Beauty," said her father.

"Just because you asked me," said Beauty, "perhaps you could bring me a rose. Because our roses aren't in flower, yet."

Don't think Beauty cared so much about roses. But she did not want to make her sisters look greedy in comparison with her, and, if she had told him she did not want a present, they would have said she only did it to show off.

So the merchant went away. But, when he arrived at the port, he found his creditors had already taken possession of the cargo and, after a deal of bother, he must go home again as poor as he had been when he set out.

He was no more than thirty miles from home and already cheerfully thinking how he would soon see his dear children again, when he lost himself in a great wood. A storm of snow came on, with such a furious wind that, twice, he was blown from his horse. When night approached, he thought that either he would die of hunger and cold or else be eaten by the wolves he could hear howling all around him.

Then, all at once at the end of a long avenue of trees, he saw a light and, as he went towards it, saw it came streaming out of the windows of a splendid palace. Thankfully, the merchant hurried forward. He was surprised to find the palace courtyard was empty, but his horse saw how the stable door stood open and promptly went inside, where the poor, famished animal at once began to munch hay and oats that looked as though they might have been specially prepared for it.

The merchant made sure his horse was comfortable and went into the house. Still nobody to be seen! But, in the great hall, a good fire, and a table, groaning with good things, at which was laid one single place. He was soaked to the skin with rain and snow and started drying himself by the fire, saying to himself: "Surely the master of the house will forgive me for taking liberties with his premises! I'm sure he'll be here soon."

He waited, and waited; but, by the time the clock struck eleven, neither the master nor so much as a single servant had appeared, and the merchant was so hungry that he seized hold of a roast chicken and disposed of it in two mouthfuls. Then he washed down the chicken with a glass of wine, and, after another glass, grew bold enough to explore. He passed through several magnificently furnished reception rooms before he found a room with a good bed in it. It was well after midnight and he was exhausted. He took a chance. He closed the door and lay down to sleep.

He did not wake until late next morning and was astonished to discover a handsome, new suit of clothes laid out for him instead of his own, old, travel-stained, weather-stained ones. "The palace must belong to a good fairy who has taken pity on me," he thought.

He looked out of the window and found the snow was gone and the park was full of flowers. Returning to the room in which he had eaten his supper, he found a pot of hot chocolate on a little table. "Thank you, good fairy!" he said out loud. "How nice of you to think of my breakfast!"

He drank up his chocolate and went to the stable for his horse. As he passed by a rose tree, he remembered the promise he had made to his Beauty, reached up, and broke off a branch of flowers.

Then there came the most terrible roaring and suddenly he saw before him a beast so hideous that he almost fainted.

"Ungrateful wretch!" said the Beast, in a terrible voice. "I saved your life and opened my home to you and now you thank me by stealing my roses, my roses that I love more than anything in the world. Only death

can pay for such a crime. I give you a quarter of an hour in which to prepare to meet your maker."

The merchant threw himself on his knees before the Beast, wringing his hands and crying: "Forgive me, sir! I didn't know I was offending you when I picked the rose my daughter asked me for!"

"Nobody calls me 'sir'," growled the Beast. "My name is Beast. I don't like compliments. I don't care what anybody thinks of me and flattery will get you nowhere. But now you tell me you have a houseful of daughters at home. I would like to forgive you—but only on this condition, that one of your daughters comes here of her own free will, to die in your place. Don't argue with me; go. And, if your daughters refuse to die for you, swear to me you will be back in three months' time."

The merchant had no intention of sacrificing one of his precious girls to this fearful creature but he thought: "At least I shall be able to hold them in my arms again, for one last time."

So he promised he would return and then the Beast softened a little. "I don't want my guest to leave empty handed," he said. "In the room where you slept, you will find an empty chest. Fill it up to the brim with whatever you see that pleases you most and I will have it delivered to your home."

With that, the Beast departed and the merchant told himself: "If I must die, then at least I know my children won't starve."

In his bedroom, he found a heap of golden guineas and put them in the chest of which the Beast had spoken, closed it and left the palace in as much distress as he had entered it with joy. He let his horse find its own way home. His children came running to welcome him but he saw them through his tears. He still carried Beauty's roses, and when he gave them to her, he said: "Take your roses, Beauty. They cost your old father very dearly." And then he told them his sad adventure.

The eldest sisters shrieked out loud and forthwith fell to blaming Beauty for everything, while Beauty sat silent and dry-eyed.

"That little flibberty-gibbet and her vanity are the cause of all this!" they said. "Why couldn't she have asked for pretty clothes, like we did! But no! Madame wanted to be different. Now she's got Daddy into this awful fix and look at her, she's not even sorry."

"Crying won't help," said Beauty. "Besides, why should I cry for my father's fate when that fate can be averted? If the Beast will take a daughter instead of the father, then I shall gladly go instead."

"Oh, no, you won't!" declared her three brothers. "We won't let you! We'll go and find this monster and he can kill us if we don't kill him first!"

"I shouldn't count on that," said the merchant. "The Beast has great powers and I do not think he could be done away with very easily. Beauty, you are too good to me. I don't want you to do this for me. I am old and have almost lived my life out. All my regrets are at leaving you, my dears."

"All the same, I certainly won't let you go off to the Beast's palace by yourself!" said Beauty. "You can't stop me following you. Young I may be, but how could I spend the rest of my life full of remorse because I caused my father's death?"

Nothing could shake Beauty. She was determined. She insisted she would go to the Beast's palace with him and her sisters were delighted to think they would be rid of her, because they were so jealous of her. The merchant was so overwhelmed with grief to think that he might lose his Beauty that he forgot the chest he had filled with gold, but, when he went to his room that night, there it was, in the space between the bed and the wall. He confided the secret to Beauty, who told him how two young men had come courting her sisters while he was away. She begged her father to let them marry. She wished her sisters well although they hated her.

Those bad girls rubbed their eyes with onions to summon up a few artificial tears when they said goodbye to Beauty, but her brothers wept from full hearts. Only Beauty seemed unmoved, but that was because she did not want them all to feel even worse.

The horse found its way back to the palace. They arrived at nightfall and, just as the merchant had first seen them, they saw the lights at the end of the avenue. The horse settled down in the stable once again in solitary

splendour and the merchant took his daughter to the great hall, where, as before, they found a laden table at which, this time, two places were set, not one. The merchant had lost his appetite but Beauty forced herself to be calm, sat down and served herself, although she could not help thinking: "The Beast must want to fatten me up before he eats me, that's why he's laid out such a spread."

When dinner was over, they heard the dreadful noise of the approaching Beast. Beauty could not keep from shuddering when she saw the Beast first, but she put on a brave face and, when he asked her if she had come to the palace of her own free will, she told him: "Yes," although she trembled.

"You are very obliging," said the Beast. "I am deeply touched. As for you, my good man, you must leave tomorrow morning and make sure you never come back. Goodnight, Beauty."

"Goodnight, Beast," she replied.

With that, he left them. The merchant took his daughter in his arms.

"I'm half dead with terror already," he said. "Leave me here, I beg you."

"Certainly not, father," said Beauty, firmly. "You shall and will go home tomorrow morning and heaven will protect me."

They went to bed and, though both thought they would not be able to sleep a wink, no sooner were they between the sheets than their eyes

closed. While she slept, Beauty dreamed a beautiful lady came to visit her and said: "Your sacrifice has made me very happy, Beauty. Don't think you shall go unrewarded."

When she woke up, she told her father about her dream and that consoled him a little, although when he left her he cried aloud in sorrow.

Now she was alone, Beauty broke down herself, for the first time. But, because she was very brave, she quickly dried her eyes, put her faith in providence and decided it would never do to spend her last hours on earth moping and moaning. She guessed the Beast must take his meals in the evenings, as animals do, and she would pass the waiting hours in exploring his palace.

Everything was so beautiful she could not stop herself wondering at it. Then, to her astonishment, she discovered a door above which was written: "Beauty's room." When she opened the door, the splendour inside dazzled her. She examined the room more closely and she found a big bookcase, a harpsichord and many volumes of music.

"Somebody doesn't want me to be bored," she said to herself. "If I have only one day left to live, surely they wouldn't have gone to so much trouble to get a room ready for me."

It was an encouraging thought. She opened the bookcase, took out a book and there she saw, on the cover, written in gold letters, the message: "Ask for whatever you wish. Here you are mistress of everything."

"But all I want is to see my father and find out what he's doing," she thought wistfully.

She did not speak out loud so imagine her surprise when, glancing in a mirror, there she saw, as if reflected, her own house and her sad-faced father dismounting from his horse. Her sisters came out to meet him, making all kinds of tragic grimaces but, all the same, they could not hide their glee to know Beauty was gone. A moment later, everything disappeared.

Beauty thought the Beast was very considerate and that, perhaps, there was nothing to fear from him, after all.

At twelve o'clock, she found the table was ready for her, and sweet music played all through her dinner, although the musicians themselves remained invisible. That evening, however, as she sat down to her supper, she heard the roaring of the Beast and could not keep from trembling.

"May I sit here and watch you eat your supper, Beauty?" he asked.

"You are the master in your own house," Beauty replied, though her voice shook.

"Not at all," said the Beast. "You must give the orders, here. If my company embarrasses you, you have only to tell me so and I will go away. Tell me, don't you think I'm very ugly?"

"Yes, I do," said Beauty, "for I cannot tell a lie. But I think you are very kind, too."

"Well, yes," said the Beast. "But, as well as being so very ugly, I'm also very slow-witted. A fool, in fact."

"A real fool would be the last person to admit that!" said Beauty. "You can't be so very stupid, after all."

"Eat up your supper, Beauty," said the Beast. "And try to amuse yourself in your house—for everything here is yours, now, and I would not like to think you were unhappy."

"That's very good of you," said Beauty. "I must say, I'm very pleased to find your rough exterior hides such a good heart. When I think of how kind you are, you seem less ugly, somehow."

"Oh, yes! I've got a good heart," said the Beast. "But all the same, I'm a monster."

"Many men are worse than you," said Beauty. "I like you better, with that ugly face of yours, than I would if you had a handsome face and wicked ways."

"If I were clever enough, I would pay you a beautiful compliment for saying that," said the Beast. "But I am a fool and all I can say is, thank you."

Beauty ate a hearty supper. She was no longer in the least afraid of the Beast, until he asked her: "Beauty, will you be my wife?" Then she was seized with terror in case the Beast fell into a rage when she refused him. But at last, her voice shaking again, she said: "No, Beast."

Then the poor Beast expelled his breath in what, if he had been a man, would have been a mournful sigh, but, since he was a beast, came out as a loud hiss, that echoed and re-echoed dolefully through the palace. But Beauty was reassured to find that he said no more than: "Then, goodnight, Beauty," and left the room, although he turned back to look at her again and again before he closed the door behind him. When he was gone, Beauty felt sorry for the Beast. "What a shame! To be so ugly, outside, and so fine, within!"

She spent three contented months in the palace. Every evening, the Beast came to visit her, to chat with her while she ate her supper, and though he was by no means a witty or a brilliant conversationalist, he always talked good, plain, common sense. Every day, Beauty found she liked more and more things about him. She soon grew used to his ugliness and, far from feeling apprehensive before his visits, she often caught herself looking at the clock to see when nine o'clock would come, because the Beast always arrived precisely then.

Only one thing preyed on Beauty's mind. Every night, before he went off, the Beast asked her if she would marry him, and he always gave his doleful sigh when she refused. At last she said firmly: "You're beginning to annoy me, Beast. I truly should like to be able to marry you but I am too sincere to let you run away with the notion it could ever be. I shall always be your friend. You must learn to be content with that."

"What must be, must be," said the Beast. "I know that I am very hideous, but I love you very much. And if you would only stay here with me forever, then my happiness would be complete. Promise you will never leave me."

Beauty blushed scarlet when she heard that. She had seen in the mirror how her father pined for her so much that he had taken to his bed and she longed to comfort him.

"I could easily promise that!" she said. "But I want to visit my father so

much that I will die of grief if you don't let me go!"

"I'd rather cut off my right paw than cause you pain," said the Beast. "I will send you home to your father. But once you are there, there you will stay—and your Beast will fade away from loneliness."

"Oh, no!" said Beauty, near tears. "I love you too much to let you do that. I promise you I will come back at the end of seven days. You let me see how my sisters are married and my brothers have gone off to join the army. My father's chicks are all flown. Let me comfort him for just one week."

"You shall be there tomorrow morning," said the Beast. "But don't forget your promise. All you need do when you want to come back to me is to put this ring down on the table beside you when you go to sleep. Goodbye."

He sighed, and Beauty went to bed in a melancholy mood at leaving him in such low spirits. But, when she woke up next morning, she found, to her delight, that she was in her father's house.

She rang the bell and a maid came running. The maid screamed with surprise at finding Beauty there, in bed, in her nightdress, and the scream brought Beauty's father. He hugged and kissed his daughter for a good quarter of an hour, he was so glad to see her safe and sound. After the first transports of joy were over, Beauty remembered she had no clothes to put on, but the maid reported the presence of a strange trunk in the hall, and this trunk was full of dresses made of cloth of gold embroidered with diamonds. The Beast thought of everything.

Beauty took out the least showy of her dresses and told the maid to lock away the rest, because she wanted to give them to her sisters, as presents. But no sooner had she said that than the trunk and all it contained vanished clean away.

"I think the Beast wants you to keep them all," said Beauty's father, and, whoosh! back everything came in an instant.

While Beauty got ready for the day, her father sent for her sisters, who brought their husbands to meet her. Both sisters were dissatisfied. The eldest sister's husband was the handsomest man you could imagine, but he was so vain he primped in front of a mirror from morning to night and did not give his wife a chance to look at herself. The second sister's husband was clever as could be, but showed off all the time by making elaborate insults, and his wife was his favourite target.

When they saw Beauty dressed like a princess, smiling like the morning, her sisters felt quite ill. Beauty kissed them and made much of them but nothing could smother their jealousy, that grew by leaps and bounds when she told them how happy she was. They escaped into the garden, there to eat their hearts out with envy.

"Why on earth is that wretched creature better off than we are?" whined one sister. "Aren't we both much more attractive than she is?"

"Darling, I have an idea," said the other sister. "Let's try to keep her here after her week's holiday is over. That idiotic Beast will be so furious with her if she breaks her word that, perhaps . . . he will gobble her up."

"What a cunning scheme!" said the first sister. "The worst of it is, having to pretend to be nice to her!"

They hurried back to the house and covered Beauty with caresses. They behaved so lovingly towards her that she could scarcely believe her eyes. When the week was up, her sisters tore their hair and set up such a wailing at the prospect of her departure that she promised to stay with them for one week more.

Yet Beauty was guilty because she knew the Beast, whom she loved dearly, was waiting anxiously for her return and, besides, she found that she was missing him very much. On the tenth night she spent in her father's house, she dreamed she was back in the garden of the Beast's

palace and the Beast himself lay at her feet on the grass, at the point of death. She woke up, shocked.

"Aren't I a wicked girl, to give such heartache to a Beast who is so good to me? Is it his fault he was born so ugly and so slow-witted? He is *good*, and that is worth all the rest put together. If I were to marry him, I would be much happier than my sisters are with *their* husbands. A woman doesn't need a handsome face and a clever tongue in a husband. She needs strength of character, goodness and kindness, and these the Beast has, all three. I am not in the least in love with him but I respect him. I feel friendship for him. I am grateful to him. I mustn't break his heart or else I shall reproach myself for the rest of my life."

Beauty got up and laid her ring down on the table. She fell fast asleep at once and, when she woke next morning, she was in the Beast's palace. She dressed herself up in the most magnificent of the clothes he had given her, in order to please him, and she could hardly bear the dreary way the day dragged by until nine o'clock came round.

The clock struck; but no Beast appeared.

Then Beauty was scared. She ran through the palace, calling for him. She was in despair. She searched everywhere until, remembering her dream, she ran out into the garden and found him where she had dreamed she would, stretched out unconscious on the grass beside a stream. She did not flinch from his ugliness but threw herself upon him and, when she found his heart still beating, brought water from the stream and bathed his face.

The Beast opened his eyes and said: "You forgot your promise to me. When you did not come back to me, I could not eat, and now I am dying, Beauty. But I shall die happy, because I have seen you again."

"No, Beast! Don't die! Live, and marry me! From this moment, I am yours, and yours alone. I thought I felt nothing but friendship for you but now I'm so unhappy that I know I cannot live without you."

As soon as she said that, the palace blazed with lights, fireworks exploded and music began to play as though a festival had just begun. But Beauty scarcely spared these wonders a glance, she was so concerned for her dear Beast. Yet what a surpise! For her Beast was gone and, at her feet instead of him, lay a handsome young prince, thanking her profusely for freeing him from the spell he had been under. Although this prince was worth all her undivided attention, still she puzzled: "What has happened to my Beast?"

"You see him before you," said the prince. "A bad fairy condemned me to the Beast's shape until I found a beautiful girl who would agree to marry me. And she forbade me to use my brilliant intellectual gifts to help my courtship, too! Only you in all the world saw my true worth under my disguise, Beauty, and the crown I offer you now is not the half of all you deserve."

Beauty, pleasantly surprised, helped the prince up from the grass and they went to the palace, where they found Beauty's entire family brought there to share her happiness by the lovely lady she had seen in the dream of her first night with the Beast. This lady was a very important fairy.

"Beauty," said the fairy, "now receive your reward. You chose virtue above good looks and quick wits and you deserve to find all these qualities united in one person. You are going to become a great queen. I hope it does not make you proud."

Then she turned to Beauty's sisters.

"As for you, ladies, I know your secrets and your maliciousness. I am going to turn you into statues. But, under your stony surfaces, you shall still keep all your human feelings. You will stand on their side of your sister's palace door and your punishment is this: every day, you will be forced to see how happy she is, and say nothing. You can turn back into your former selves just as soon as either one of you is prepared to admit that neither is entirely perfect but, knowing you as I do, I think you are probably doomed to be statues forever, for nothing short of a miracle can cure an envious disposition."

Then the fairy struck her ring and all those present were instantly transported to the prince's kingdom, where they were greeted with cheers and thanksgiving. The prince married Beauty and they lived happily ever after, in a contentment perfect because it was founded on goodness.

The Fairies

There once lived an old widow who had two daughters. The eldest was the living image of her mother to look at, and worse, to listen to; they were both so proud and disagreeable it was impossible to live with them. But the youngest took after her father in gentleness and kindness and she was also very, very beautiful. Because it is only natural to love people like oneself, the widow adored her eldest daughter and could scarcely stand the sight of the youngest one, who had to have her meals all by herself in the kitchen while the others ate in the dining room, and she made her slave away at all the household chores, too.

Twice a day, she had to go and fetch water from a spring half a mile from the house and bring home a brimming pitcherful. One day, when she went to the spring, she found an old woman there who begged her for a drink.

"Oh yes, indeed!" said the lovely girl with alacrity. She rinsed out her pitcher and dipped it into the spring just where it bubbled out freshly from the rock; and she held the pitcher carefully so that the old woman could drink from it in comfort.

Now, this old woman was really a fairy who had assumed the form of a poor peasant in order to test the girl's good heart. As soon as she finished her drink, she said:

"You are so beautiful, so good and so kind that I feel I must give you a special present. My fairy gift is this: at each word you say, either a flower or else a precious stone will fall out of your mouth."

When the lovely girl arrived home, how they berated her for staying so long at the fountain!

"Mother, dear, I beg your pardon," said the girl and out of her mouth dropped two roses, two pearls and two fat diamonds.

"What do I see before me?" cried her mother. "I could have sworn I saw pearls and diamonds dropping out of her mouth! What can you have been up to, my dear?"

It was the first time in all her life she'd used an endearment towards her younger daughter. The girl told her mother exactly what had happened, scattering a great many diamonds as she did so.

"I must send my eldest girl to the well at once," said the widow. "Fanchon, just look at what comes out of your sister's mouth whenever she opens it! Wouldn't you like to be the same? All you have to do is to go and fetch the water from the spring and give some to the poor woman who'll ask you for a drink."

"I'd like to see myself going off to the spring like a slavey!" snapped the ugly one.

"Go you shall; and this very minute," her mother snapped back.

So off she went but she grumbled all the way and she would not take a common pitcher but armed herself with the best silver jug in the house. No sooner had she arrived at the spring than a fine lady dressed in the height of fashion came out of the woods and asked if she could drink from her jug. This lady was the very same fairy who had appeared to her sister, but now she put on the manners of a princess in order to find out just how rude Fanchon could be.

"Haven't I dragged myself all the way here just to give you a drink of water?" whined Fanchon. "Haven't I lugged this silver flagon all the way from home expressly for madame's drinking convenience? Oh, yes, that's why I've come; drink, if you want to, you've caused me quite enough bother."

The fairy did not lose her temper.

"Nobody could call you a nice woman," she said coolly. "Since you are so disobliging, I shall disoblige you with a most inconvenient present; every time you say one single word, you'll shed either a toad or a snake from your uncivil lips."

When her mother saw Fanchon coming home, she cried:

"How did it go?"

"It's all your fault!" whined the ugly one, and out of her mouth fell two vipers and a pair of toads.

"Heavens above, what do I see?" cried her mother. "Your sister is responsible for this. I'll pay her back!"

She hurried off to find her, to beat her, and the poor child ran away into the neighbouring forest to save herself. The king's son met her as he came home from his hunting. When he saw how pretty she was, he asked her what she was doing in the woods all by herself; and why was she crying so?

"Alas, kind sir! My own mother has driven me away from home!"

The prince saw five or six pearls and just as many diamonds come tumbling out of her mouth when she spoke and he begged her to tell him where they came from. She told him everything.

The prince was charmed with her and decided that her remarkable talent was worth more than the dowry of any princess in the world; he took her to the palace of the king, his father, and married her.

Her sister grew so hateful that even her mother got tired of her, at last, and turned her out of doors. Try as she might, she could find nobody to take pity on her and she crept away and died in a corner of the woods.

Moral

Kindness and consideration for others may inconvenience one, in the short run; but, sooner or later, kindness reaps its rewards and often when least expected.

Another moral

Diamonds and pearls make powerful impressions; but kind words are more powerful still, and are infinitely more valuable.

Hop o' my Thumb

A certain woodcutter and his wife were blessed with seven sons. The eldest was ten years old and the youngest seven. It may seem a remarkable feat to produce so many children in so little time but the woodcutter's wife had gone to work with a will and rarely given her husband less than two at once.

They were very poor and their seven children were a great inconvenience because none of them could earn their living.

The youngest was the greatest inconvenience of all; he was a weakling and a mute, and they mistook his debility for stupidity. He was very, very tiny and when he came into the world he was scarcely bigger than your thumb. So they called him "Hop o' my Thumb".

This poor child was the butt of the household and they were always finding fault with him. But he was really the cleverest of them all and if he did not speak much, he listened very, very carefully.

At last there came a year of such terrible famine that the poor people decided they could not provide for their children any more.

One evening, when the children were in bed and the woodcutter sat

with his wife by the fire, he said to her with a breaking heart:

"You know we've got nothing to give our children to eat. I can't bear to see them die of hunger in front of my very eyes. I've decided to take them out in the woods tomorrow and lose them there. It will be very easy. While they are gathering up sticks, we'll slip away without them seeing us."

"Oh!" cried his wife. "How could you think of abandoning your own children?"

Her husband painted her a grisly picture of their plight but, all the same, she would not agree to his scheme—she was poor, but she was their mother. But then when she thought how sad she would be to see them starve to death, she said, yes; and went to bed in tears.

When Hop o' my Thumb had realised his parents were discussing something of importance, he crept from his bed and hid himself under his father's stool, to eavesdrop, so he heard everything they said. Back he went to bed but he did not sleep that night; he was planning his strategy.

He got up early and went to the bank of a stream, and filled his pockets with little white pebbles. Then he came home again. When the family set off for the wood, Hop o' my Thumb did not tell his brothers his dreadful secret.

They went to the thickest part of the forest, where you could not see another person if you were ten steps away from them. The woodcutter began to chop down a tree and the children went off to collect sticks and make them up into bundles. When their father and mother saw they were busy and happy, they edged further and further away, until they could no longer glimpse a single child: then they took to their heels and fled.

When the children found out they were all by themselves, they began to cry with all their might. Hop o' my Thumb let them cry for a while, because he knew how to get back home again. As they walked through the forest, he had let drop the little white pebbles he had kept in his pocket all along the way. Now he said to his brothers:

"Don't be scared. Mother and father have abandoned us here, but I will take you home again. Just follow me."

They trooped after him and he led them straight home by the same way they had gone into the forest. At first, they did not dare go inside the cottage, but listened at the door to find out what was going on.

As soon as the woodcutter and his wife had arrived home, the village squire sent them ten golden sovereigns he had owed them for so long they had given up hope he would ever repay the debt. The money was life to them; they were dying of hunger. The woodcutter sent his wife straight out to the butcher's. They had not eaten for so long she had forgotten how much meat to buy and bought three times as much as the two of them needed. When they sat down at the table, the woodcutter's wife lamented:

"Alas, where are our poor children now? They would have feasted off the leavings of our spread! But you would insist in getting rid of them, William; I told you we would regret it. What are they doing in the forest? Perhaps the wolves have already eaten them! What an inhuman brute you are, to abandon your children!"

If she reminded him once she reminded him twenty times how he'd regret it and at last he lost patience with her and threatened to beat her if she did not keep quiet. She was making a deafening clamour and he was the kind of man who likes a woman to speak her mind but can't stand a woman who is always right.

The woodcutter's wife was crying dreadfully.

"Alas, alas, where are my poor children?"

She cried so loudly that the children outside heard her and sang out all together:

"Here we are! Here we are!"

She ran to open the door for them and hugged and kissed them.

"Oh, my darlings, how happy I am to see you! You must be very tired, you must be very hungry . . . Oh, Pierrot! How dirty you are! Come and have your face washed!"

Pierrot was her eldest son and she loved him more than all the others because he had ginger hair and her own hair was on the carroty side, too.

They sat down and ate so much their mother and father were filled with joy. They told their parents how scary the forest had been, interrupting one another and all talking at once. The woodcutter and his wife were delighted to have their children home with them and the joy lasted exactly as long as the ten golden sovereigns. But when the money was all gone, they began to despair and decided, once again, to leave the children to their fates. But this time there would be no mistake. They would take the children twice as far from home before they abandoned them, so they could never return.

But they could not plot secretly enough to stop Hop o' my Thumb hearing them and he made it his business to organise things as he had done before. But when he got up at dawn to go and fetch his pebbles, his scheme came to nothing, for he found the door of the house securely locked. He did not know what to do until the woodcutter's wife gave each of them a piece of bread for their lunch.

Then he thought he would be able to use breadcrumbs instead of pebbles to scatter behind him along the way, so he stored his bread in his pocket.

Their father and mother took them to the densest, darkest part of the forest and once they had arrived, they slipped away through the undergrowth and left the children behind. Hop o' my Thumb did not worry very much, at first, because he thought he could easily find his way home because of the track of breadcrumbs he had scattered as he walked; but he was astonished to discover he could not find a single crumb when he started to look for them, because the birds had come and eaten them all.

Now they were in a sorry state. The more they searched for the way home, the more they lost themselves in the forest. Night came on and brought a great wind with it, so they were very much afraid. They thought they heard the howling of wolves who had come to devour them. They hardly dared speak. Then it began to rain and they were soaked through. They slithered in the mud at every step, fell down and dragged themselves to their feet again, filthy from head to toe.

Hop o' my Thumb climbed up a tree to see if he could discover anything about their surroundings. He looked about on all sides until he saw a little glimmer of light like the light from a candle, far off in the forest. When he came down from his perch, he could see nothing but he made his brothers trudge off in the direction of the light and, after a while, they saw it again as they came out of the wood.

At last they arrived at the house with the candle in the window, not without more alarms—they often lost sight of the light and fell into holes several times. They knocked at the door and a woman answered it. She asked them what they wanted.

"We are poor children lost in the forest," replied Hop o' my Thumb. "Can we beg a bed for the night, in the name of charity?"

The woman saw how pretty they were and began to weep.

"Oh, you poor children, why have you come? Don't you know who lives here? A horrid ogre, who eats babies."

Hop o' my Thumb shook with fear, like his brothers, but he said:

"Oh, kind lady, what shall we do? If you don't let us into your house, the wolves in the forest will certainly eat us. And on the whole, we would very much rather be eaten by the ogre than by the wolves, because the ogre might take pity on us, especially if you ask him to."

The ogre's wife thought she would be able to hide them until the next morning, so she let them in and took them to warm themselves beside a good fire where a whole sheep was turning on a spit for the ogre's supper.

74

While they were thawing out, they heard three or four great bangs at the door; the ogre had come home. The ogre's wife hid them under the bed and went to let him in. The ogre asked if his supper was ready and his wine drawn from the barrel; then he sat down at the table. The sheep was still turning on the spit but he thought he smelled something better than roast mutton. He snuffed the air to the right and he snuffed the air to the left; he said he smelled fresh meat.

"Why, that must be the calf I was just going to skin!" said his wife.

"I smell fresh meat, I tell you," repeated the ogre, looking at his wife suspiciously. "And something is going on that I don't understand."

He got up and went straight to the bed.

"So you wanted to trick me, did you, you old cow! I don't know why I don't eat you, too, but I daresay you'd be too tough. Here's some game delivered to me at just the right time— the very thing to give my three ogrish friends for dinner tomorrow!"

One after the other, he pulled the poor children from under the bed. They fell to their knees and begged his pardon but they had fallen into the hands of the cruellest of ogres, who, far from taking pity on them, was

75

already eating them up with his eyes and telling his wife they were such delicious morsels that she would have to make an especially good sauce to go with them.

He got out an enormous knife and began to sharpen it on a long stone, under the terrified gaze of Hop o' my Thumb and his brothers. But when he seized hold of Pierrot, his wife said:

"What can you be thinking of, slaughtering at this hour? Won't there be enough time tomorrow?"

"Keep your mouth shut," said the ogre. "I like my game well hung."

"But goodness me, isn't there enough meat in the house already? There's a calf, two sheep and the best part of a pig."

"Oh, very well, then," said the ogre. "Give them some supper to fatten them up and put them to bed."

The ogre's wife was overjoyed and took them plenty of supper but they were too frightened to eat it. As for the ogre, he sat down to some serious drinking to celebrate his pleasure at finding such delicious fare with which to entertain his friends. He put away twice as much good wine as usual and it went to his head, so he stretched out on his bed for a nap.

The ogre had seven little daughters who all had wonderfully fresh complexions because they ate so much fresh meat, just like their father. But besides their rosy cheeks, they had nasty little round grey eyes, hooked noses and enormous mouths with long green teeth sharpened to a point, and those teeth had huge gaps between them. They were still too young to be very wicked but they showed signs of great promise and had already taken to biting babies in order to suck their blood.

The horrid little things had all been sent to bed early and were lying, all seven, in one bed, and each wore a golden crown on her head. There was another bed just the same size in their room and the ogre's wife put the seven boys to sleep in it before she went to lie down beside her husband.

Hop o' my Thumb saw the golden crowns on the heads of the little

ogresses. He was afraid the ogre might wake up in the night and want to get on with his butchering; after a while, Hop o' my Thumb got up and took the caps off the heads of his brothers. He crept across the room and took the crowns from the heads of the baby ogresses. He put the crowns on his brothers' heads and one on his own, and put their caps on the baby ogresses, so that the ogre would think the woodcutter's sons were his own daughters and the girls were really the boys.

About midnight, the ogre woke up and was seized with regret that he had left till the morrow a task he might have performed that day. He jumped out of bed and picked up his big knife.

"Let's go and have another look at those funny little objects," he said to himself.

He tiptoed into his daughters' bedroom and went to the bed where the little boys slept soundly, except for Hop o' my Thumb, who was very frightened when the ogres hands groped at his face. But when the ogre touched the golden crown he wore, he said:

"Why, what a nasty trick I almost played on myself! I must have had a drop too much last night."

So off he went to the other bed and felt for the boys' caps.

"Here they are, the little lambs!" he cried. "Let's fall to work."

With that, he slit the throats of his seven daughters. Well content with the night's work, he went back to bed again.

As soon as Hop o' my Thumb heard the ogre start to snore, he woke up his brothers and told them to put their clothes on and follow him. They went into the garden as quietly as they could and jumped over the wall. Shaking with terror, they ran through the night without even knowing where they were going.

When the ogre woke up in the morning, he said to his wife:

"Go down below and get those little fellows from last night ready."

The ogre's wife was surprised and pleased because she thought he meant "get them ready for the day", not "get them ready for the pot". She thought he had taken pity on them. So upstairs she went, and found her seven daughters, with their throats cut, swimming in blood.

She responded with a fainting fit; most women faint in similar circumstances. The ogre thought his wife had been away long enough and climbed up the stairs to see what the matter was. He was no less astonished than his wife at the spectacle which awaited him.

"What have I done?" he cried. "I'll pay the rascals back for the trick they played me, and pay them back quickly!"

He threw a bucket of water over his wife to bring her round and when she came to he said:

"Quick, get me my seven-league boots so that I can go and catch those criminals!"

He raced across the country until he came to the lane where the poor children were running, and now they were only a hundred yards from their own father's door. They saw the ogre striding from mountain to mountain, and skipping across rivers as if they were streams. Hop o' my Thumb spied a crack in a nearby rock and quickly hid his six brothers there. He tucked himself in beside them, peering out to keep an eye on the ogre. The ogre was weary after his long, useless search; besides, seven-league boots are very exhausting to wear. He wanted a sit down and, as luck would have it, he parked himself on the very rock in which the little boys were hiding.

He was so tired that soon he fell asleep and began to snore so frightfully that the poor children were just as frightened as they had been when he was flourishing his big knife ready to cut their throats. But Hop o' my Thumb told his brothers to run home while the giant was sound asleep and not to bother about him, because he could take care of himself. So off they ran.

Hop o' my Thumb went up to the ogre, took the boots off his feet so gently he did not wake him, and put them on himself. The boots were very long and very large but, since they were of fairy make, they could swell or shrink according to the size of the foot that wore them.

Hop o' my Thumb went to the ogre's house straight away. The ogre's wife was weeping beside the corpses of her daughters.

"Your husband is in terrible danger," announced Hop o' my Thumb. "He has been captured by a gang of robbers who say they will kill him if he doesn't give them all his money. As they held the knife to his throat, he noticed me standing discreetly by and begged me to come straight to you and tell you to give me everything he owns and not keep back a penny.

Otherwise, the robbers will kill him without mercy. He told me to borrow his seven-league boots because the matter was so pressing, and to prove to you I was no imposter, too.

The good woman was terrified and quickly gave him all she had, because the ogre was a good husband in spite of his daily diet of young children, and she wanted to save him. Hop o' my Thumb, loaded with the ogre's treasure, took himself off to his father's house, where he had the most joyful welcome.

Some people disagree with this ending—they say that Hop o' my Thumb never robbed the ogre and the truth of it was, that he only took the seven-league boots. These people claim they know the true facts and, to clinch the matter, go so far as to say they have even enjoyed the hospitality of the woodcutter's own home. They say that when Hop o' my Thumb put on the ogre's boots, he went to the king's court because he knew an enemy army was camped two miles away and all at the capital were agog to know the results of the latest battle. They say he went to the king and asked him if he wanted full military reports before sunset. The king promised him a great deal of money for the information and Hop o' my Thumb brought back the news that very evening. After that, the king paid him handsomely to carry orders to the army; besides, a great many ladies paid him any price he cared to name for news of their lovers. He made his greatest profits from this activity.

One or two married women also hired him to send letters to their husbands but they paid very badly and provided very little business; it was a poor thing in comparison.

He worked as a special messenger until he saved up a small fortune. Then he went home to his father's house. He took good care of his entire family; he brought peerages for his father and all his brothers and lived in ease and comfort for the rest of his life.

Moral

It is no affliction to have a large family if they are all handsome, strong and clever. But if one of them is a puny weakling, he will be despised, jeered at and mocked. However, often the runt of the litter ends up making the family fortune.

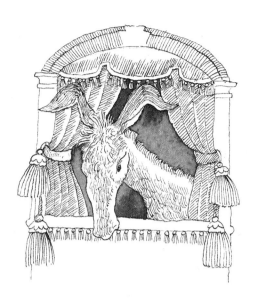

Donkey-Skin

Once upon a time, there lived a wise and happy king, who had a beautiful wife, a lovely daughter, a magnificent palace, wise and capable ministers, virtuous and devoted courtiers, faithful and hard-working servants and vast stables filled with the finest horses. But everyone who visited those stables was astonished to see how an ugly old donkey with very long ears looked at its ease in the most sumptuous stall of all. There was more to this beast than met the eye, however; he was well worth all the care the king could give him because, every morning, he covered his litter, not with dung, but with many, many golden coins.

One day, the queen fell sick and no doctor could cure her. The whole country mourned. When she felt her last hour approaching, the queen said to her weeping husband:

"Promise me one thing, before I die; promise me you will marry again."

The king let out a piteous cry, clasped hold of her hands, bathed them with tears and told her he would never so much as think of taking another wife. But the queen said firmly:

"You must and you will marry again. All your ministers will say you

81

must, because I have only given you a daughter and they will say you need sons, to inherit the kingdom. But I beg you, by all the love you have for me, not to marry again until you have found a princess more beautiful than I. Give me your word and I will die happy."

The queen was very vain and did not believe there could possibly be another woman in the world as beautiful as she was, so she thought she had cunningly ensured the king could never marry again at all and died happy. No husband ever made more fuss, weeping, sobbing day and night; but great sorrows do not last long. Besides, all his ministers of state came in a body to see him, just as the queen had said they would, and told him that wedlock was his duty.

The king burst into tears again and reminded them of the promise he had made to the queen, but his ministers said: be that as it may, he owed his country another queen, a live one.

So the king started to look for a suitable fiancée. Every day, he studied charming portraits of suitable princesses but not one of them was half as pretty as his dead queen had been. Then he looked at his own daughter and saw she had grown up. Now she was even lovelier than her mother had been when the king first met her and he fell head over heels in love with her and proposed. The princess was filled with horror. She threw herself at her father's feet and pleaded with him to see reason but the king had set his heart on this strange project, because only by marrying his daughter could he keep the promise he had made to his wife and please his ministers, too. He ordered the girl to obey him.

The young princess decided it was high time she consulted her god-mother, the Lilac Fairy, and went off to visit her that very night in a little carriage drawn by a wise sheep who knew all the back alleys of fairyland. The Lilac Fairy, most loving of godmothers, knew already, by magic, what had happened; she told the princess that nothing could harm her if she did what she was told.

"Tell your father you won't marry him unless he gives you a dress that is exactly the colour of the sky. However much he loves you, he will never be able to do that."

The princess thanked her godmother and went home. Next morning, she told her father, the king, that she would not listen to another word from him until he brought her a dress the colour of the sky. The king assembled the finest dressmakers in the kingdom and asked them to make

just such a dress. And if they failed, they would be hanged, every one of them.

Next morning, much to the princess' embarrassment, a dress the very colour of a summer sky full of golden clouds was ready and waiting for her. The king said that now she must marry him; and off she went, again, to her godmother, who told her, this time, to ask for a dress that was the colour of the moon. The king could refuse his darling nothing. He sent for the dressmakers and ordered a dress just like the moon, to be ready in twenty-four hours exactly.

The princess looked at her marvellous new dress, the colour of moonlight, and wept. At that moment, the Lilac Fairy arrived in person to comfort her.

"I think that if you asked for a dress the colour of the sun, we might outwit your father," she said.

So the princess asked for a dress the colour of the sun. The king took all the diamonds and rubies from his crown to ornament this wonderful garment. Nothing was spared; he emptied all his coffers. When the dress was finished, the dressmakers had to shut their eyes, it was so dazzling; that is why dark glasses were invented. The princess had never seen such wonderful workmanship and she was overcome. She said the dress shone so brightly it had given her a headache and retreated to her room, where the Lilac Fairy was waiting for her. The Lilac Fairy was very angry indeed.

"I know your father is quite determined to marry you but I think he would be very stupid indeed if he does as I shall tell you to ask him, now. Ask him for the skin of the donkey who fills his treasury for him. Go at once and ask him."

The princess thought her father would never sacrifice his magic donkey and so she asked for the donkey's skin. The king did not think twice about it; the poor beast was slaughtered that very day and he brought the skin to the princess himself. Now there was no way out. The princess wept and tore her hair but the resourceful Lilac Fairy comforted her.

"Wrap yourself up in the donkey-skin, run away from the palace and go wherever your fortune takes you. God will protect you because you are such a good girl. Off you go; and I will send you your lovely dresses after you. Wherever you may be, your trunk, with all your clothes and jewels in it, will speed after you under the ground. Here! I shall give you my ring. Strike the ground when you need your baggage and there it will be. Now

run along quickly, don't dally."

The princess kissed her godmother, wrapped herself in the donkey-skin, smeared her face with soot from the chimney and went out of the palace without anybody recognising her.

The flight of the princess caused a great uproar. The king had already prepared a magnificent wedding and he was in despair. He sent hundreds of soldiers out to search for her but her godmother cast a cloak of invisibility over her so they never found her, and he was left all alone.

The princess went far, very far and then still further, looking for a lodging, but though the village people gave her food, for charity's sake, she was so ugly and dirty nobody would give her a home. At last she came to a fine city and found a farm outside the city gates where the farmer needed a scullery maid, to wash the dishes, feed the turkeys and watch the sheep. When they saw the poor traveller, they asked her in and the princess was glad of it, for she was very tired. She was given a little corner by the kitchen stove where she was the butt of all the jokes of the farm-hands for the first few days, because of her dirty face and the donkey-skin wrapped around her. But they soon got used to her and she did her duties so well the farmer and his wife grew fond of her and took good care of her. Soon she was tending the sheep and turkeys as if she had never done anything else in her life.

For a long time, she never took off her disguise at all but, one day, after she had washed her face and her hands in a little spring and saw how her skin was still fresh and blooming, her hands white and smooth, although she worked so hard, she was so pleased to find she was still beautiful that she washed herself all over. When she was clean again, she could hardly bear to put on her donkey-skin in order to go back to the farm. And, as luck would have it, next day was a holiday and the farm-hands went off to town to enjoy themselves; all was peace and quiet.

In the privacy of her room, she struck the Lilac Fairy's ring on the ground and, in an instant, there stood her trunk with all her dresses in it. She opened her trunk, combed her hair and put on the dress that was the colour of the sky. Her room was so small she could not spread out her blue skirts but, once again, she felt like a real princess.

She decided she would put on all her lovely dresses, turn and turn about, on Sundays and holidays, as her only little treat, and she would put jewels and flowers in her hair, too; and so she did. Every Sunday, every holiday, she would dress herself up and arrange her hair in an elaborate coiffure— and then sigh, because only the sheep and turkeys were there to see how beautiful she was and they loved her just as much when she was wearing the horrid donkey-skin that had earned her the nickname by which she was known at the farm. Donkey-Skin. They called her Donkey-Skin.

One Sunday, when Donkey-Skin happened to have dressed herself up in the dress that was the colour of the sun, the son of the king of that country, who owned the farm, got down from his horse to rest there on his way home from hunting. This prince was young, strong and handsome, the apple of his father's eye. The farmer offered him the best in the house and, after he had eaten and drunk, the prince took a little walk round his property. He came to a dark alley with a door at the end of it and this door was tight shut. Out of curiosity, he bent down and peered through the keyhole. And, in the room, he saw such a beautiful lady in so wonderful a dress she looked like an angel just dropped from heaven. He was so struck with the sight of her he could have forced the door open and rushed inside, if she had not also instantly inspired him with the deepest respect.

He dragged himself away from the dark corner and asked the farmer who it was who lived in the little room. They told him it was the scullery maid, and she was called Donkey-Skin, because of the curious garment she wore, and she was so dirty that nobody could bear to look at her or speak

to her. They themselves had only taken her in out of pity, to look after the sheep and the turkeys.

The prince thought there was something very odd about this information but he saw that the farmer and his wife knew nothing more interesting about the girl who lived at the end of the alley and it was useless to question them any further. He went home to the king's palace beside himself with love. He wished he had knocked on the scullery maid's door and swore to himself he would do just that the next time he went to the farm. He was so much in love that he made himself ill; that very night, he was seized with a terrible fever. He was an only child and the queen, his mother, despaired when no medicine seemed to help him. The doctors did all they could but nothing made him any better.

At last, they decided he must have grown sick because of the pangs of an unsatisfied longing. They told the queen their diagnosis and she begged her son to tell her what troubled him. If he wanted to be king, then his father would gladly abdicate in his favour; if he wanted to marry, then they would even go to war to bring home for him the princess he loved. But he must not die, oh, no; for if he died, then his loving parents would die, too, of grief.

"Madame," said the prince weakly, "I am not an unnatural son. I don't want my father's crown; may he live to wear it many years more. As for marriage, I've hardly thought of it."

"Oh, my son, save the lives of your loving parents. Tell me what it is you want and you shall have it."

"What I want most in all the world . . . is that Donkey-Skin should bake me a cake and, when it is ready, she should bring it to me with her own hands."

The queen was startled to hear such an odd name; she asked who Donkey-Skin might be. One of the courtiers had caught sight of the girl at the farm and told the queen:

"It's the ugliest thing in the world, after the wolf. It's a hideous, black, wrinkled object that lives in your farmyard and looks after your turkeys."

"Never mind," said the queen. "Perhaps my son ate some of her cakes on the way back from hunting and now he has a sick fancy to eat them again. Donkey-Skin must bake him a cake immediately."

A messenger ran to the farm and asked Donkey-Skin to bake a cake for the prince as well as she knew how.

Now, some people say that Donkey-Skin saw the prince out of her little window just before he put his eyes to her keyhole, and he was so handsome she could not get him out of her mind. But whether she had seen him, or else had heard the talk about how handsome and brave he was, she was very pleased to find she had the chance to bake a cake for him. She shut herself up in her room, threw off the leathery old pelt, washed her face and hands, combed her golden hair, put on her moon-coloured dress and baked the prince a cake. She used the best flour, eggs and fresh butter. As she worked, either by accident or on purpose, she dropped a ring from her finger into the mixing bowl. When the cake was ready, she wrapped herself up in the donkey-skin again and gave the cake to the messenger. She asked for news of the prince's health but the messenger did not deign to reply; he ran off with the cake straightaway to the palace.

The prince snatched the cake from the messenger's hands and gobbled it so quickly the doctors who were present shook their heads and muttered to themselves about unhealthy appetites. Then he choked on a mouthful and took the princess' ring from his mouth. He stopped devouring the cake and examined his treasure; it was a fine emerald set in such a tiny band of gold that only one finger in the world could have been slender enough to fit it.

He kissed the ring and hid it away under his pillow, though he took it out and looked at it whenever he thought nobody was watching him. He schemed how he could meet the girl whose ring it was but he did not think they would let Donkey-Skin come to see him and he dared not tell anyone what he had seen through the keyhole in case they thought he was delirious. He worried so much that his fever returned and, this time, the doctors diagnosed love-sickness.

The king and queen sat at their son's bedside, weeping.

"Tell us the name of the one you love and, whoever she is, you shall have her," they said.

The prince replied: "Father and mother, there is an emerald ring under my pillow. I want to marry the girl to whom that ring belongs."

The king and queen took the ring, inspected it closely and decided it must belong to a lady. Then the king kissed his son and told him to get well. He ordered drums, pipes and trumpets to play all over the town and heralds to announce that anyone who wanted to try the ring should come to the palace and the girl whose finger it fitted would marry the king's son himself.

First, all the princesses in the kingdom arrived to try it on; then the duchesses, the marchionesses and the peeresses. But though they tugged and pulled at the ring, not one of them had a slender enough finger to wear it. Then they tried it on the seamstresses and though they were all very pretty, their fingers were too big, too. Then came the turn of the chamber-maids, but they had no better luck. At last the prince, who conducted all the trials himself, called for the cooks, the kitchen maids and the shepherdesses and all of them came to try the ring but their hands were so swollen with hard work the ring would not even slip over the first joint of their little fingers.

"Now it is the turn of Donkey-Skin, who baked me a cake when I was sick," said the prince. Everybody burst out laughing and said, no! how could the beautiful ring ever fit Donkey-Skin, who was so ugly and dirty.

"Go and fetch her at once," said the prince. "I mustn't leave anybody out."

Laughing uproariously, they went to fetch the girl who looked after the turkeys.

The princess heard the noise of the drums and the shouts of the heralds and she was very fearful, because she was in love with the prince; true love is humble and she was sure the ring would fit some other lady's finger and she would lose him. When the herald knocked at her door, she was full of joy. She combed her hair and put on her silver bodice with the skirt of silver lace embroidered with emeralds, but she covered all this splendour with her donkey-skin before she left her room. As the messengers from the palace led her to the prince, they mocked her cruelly and when the prince himself saw her in her ugly clothes, he could scarcely believe there might be the same girl inside them whom he had seen through the keyhole at the farm.

"Do you live in a little room at the end of a dark alley behind the farmyard?" he asked her.

"Yes, sir, I do," she replied.

"Show me your hand," he said, trembling.

Out from under that black, hideous hide came a tiny little pink and white hand and the ring slipped smoothly on to her slim finger. The princess shrugged the donkey-skin from her shoulders and there she stood in all her glory, so beautiful that the prince fell at her feet and embraced her knees with an ardour that made her blush. The king and the queen

asked her if she would like to marry their son and kissed her, too. The princess was overwhelmed and, as she stammered her thanks, the ceiling of the room opened and down came the Lilac Fairy in a chariot made of branches of lilac, and the Lilac Fairy told them the whole story of how the princess came to wear the donkey-skin.

The king and the queen were naturally delighted to learn that Donkey-Skin was a great princess and the prince loved her still more when he realised how resolute she was. He wanted to marry her so badly he could hardly wait for the banns to be called and his father and mother already adored her. But the princess declared that she could not marry the prince until she had the consent of her own father and so, according to the advice of the Lilac Fairy, who attended to everything, her father was sent a wedding invitation that did not give the name of the bride.

Kings from all over the world came to the wedding, some in sedan chairs, some in carriages. Those from furthest away arrived on elephants, on tigers or on eagles. But the greatest and most magnificent of all the kings was the father of our princess and he had mercifully quite forgotten how he had ever wanted to marry her himself. Indeed, in the meantime, he had married the lovely widow of a neighbouring king. The princess ran to meet him. He recognised her immediately and kissed her very tenderly before she had a chance to kneel before him. He gladly gave his consent to her marriage and the wedding was celebrated with all the pomp imaginable.

The king abdicated that same day and gave his throne to his son, in spite of the young man's protests. The wedding celebrations lasted for three whole months but the love of the married couple lasted longer than that—until they died.

Moral

The story of Donkey-Skin is not something you might read every day in the morning papers. But as long as there are children, mothers, grandmothers and Mother Goose, it will always seem new.

Ricky with the Tuft

There was once a queen who gave birth to a son so ugly and ungainly that even his mother's heart could not warm to him at all. But the fairy midwife who attended her told her she would certainly learn to love him because he would grow up to be very clever and exceptionally charming and, she added, because of the gift she was about to make him, he would be able to share his native wit with the one he would love best, when the time came.

So the queen was somewhat consoled for having brought such an ugly object into the world and no sooner had the child learned to speak than he began to chatter away so cleverly, and to behave with so much engaging intelligence, that everyone was charmed by him and he was universally loved. I forgot to tell you that he was born with a little tuft of hair on top of his head, which earned him the nickname: Ricky with the Tuft. Ricky was the name of his family.

At the end of seven or eight years, the queen of a neighbouring country gave birth to twin daughters. The first to be born was as beautiful as the day; the queen was so overjoyed that the nurses were afraid she might lose her senses. The same fairy midwife who had attended the birth of Ricky with the Tuft had arrived to look after this queen, too, and, to calm her excesses, she told her that, alas, the pretty little princess had no sense at all and would grow up to be as stupid as she was beautiful. The queen was very upset to hear that and even more upset, a moment or two later, when her second daughter arrived in the world and *this* one proved to be extraordinarily ugly.

"Don't distress yourself, madame," said the fairy. "Your other daughter will have many compensations. She will be so clever and witty that nobody will notice how plain she is."

"I truly hope so!" exclaimed the queen. "But isn't there any way we could give this pretty one just a spark or two of the ugly one's wit?"

"I can do nothing for her on that account," said the fairy. "But I can certainly make her more beautiful than any girl in the world. And since there is nothing I would not do to make you happy, I am going to give her the power to make whoever it is with whom she falls in love as beautiful as she is, too."

As the two princesses grew up, their perfections grew with them and everywhere nobody talked of anything but the beauty of the elder and the wit and wisdom of the younger. But age also emphasised their defects. The younger grew more ugly as you looked at her and the elder became daily more and more stupid. Either she was struck dumb the minute somebody spoke to her or else she said something very foolish in reply. Besides, she was so clumsy she could not put four pots on the mantelpiece without breaking one of them, nor drink a glass of water without spilling half of it on her clothes.

Although beauty is usually a great asset in a young woman, her younger sister always far outshone the elder in company. First of all, they would flock around the lovely one to look at her and admire her but soon she was abandoned for the company of the one with more to say for herself. And in less than a quarter of an hour, there she would be, all by herself and the younger the centre of an animated throng. However stupid the elder might be, she could not help but notice it and she would have sacrificed all her beauty without a single regret for half her sister's wit, intelligence and charm. The queen tried to prevent herself but, even so, she could not help reproaching the girl for her stupidity now and then and that made the poor princess want to die for grief.

One day, when she was hiding herself in a wood bemoaning her fate, she

saw a little man whose unprepossessing appearance was equalled only by the magnificence of his clothes. It was the young prince, Ricky with the Tuft, who had fallen head over heels in love with the pretty pictures of the princess that were on sale in all the shops. He had left his father's kingdom in order to see her in the flesh, and speak to her. He was delighted to meet her accidentally, alone in the wood, and greeted her with great respect. After he had paid her the usual compliments, he saw how sad she looked and said to her:

"Madame, I don't understand how a lady as beautiful as you are could possibly be as unhappy as you seem to be. I've had the good fortune to meet a great many beautiful people but I can truthfully say I've never seen anybody half as beautiful as you."

"You are very kind," said the princess and, since she could think of nothing more to say, she fell abruptly silent.

"Beauty is such a blessing, why! it is more important than anything," said Ricky. "And if one is beautiful, I don't understand how anything could ever upset one."

"Oh, I'd much rather be as ugly as you are and be clever than be as beautiful and as terribly, terribly stupid as me!"

"Nothing reveals true wisdom so much as the conviction one is a fool, madame; and the truly wise are those who know they are fools."

"I don't know anything about any of that," said the princess. "But I do know I really am a fool and that's the reason why I'm so unhappy."

"If that's the only reason for your unhappiness, madame, then I can cure it in a trice."

"How can you do that?" asked the princess.

"Well, madame, I have the power to dower the lady whom I love with as much wit as she wishes and, since you are the very one for me, wit and wisdom are yours for the asking if you would consent to become my wife."

The princess was utterly taken aback and could not speak a single word.

"I see my proposal throws you into a state of confusion," said Ricky with the Tuft. "That doesn't surprise me. I will give you a whole year in which to make up your mind."

The princess had so few brains and such a longing to possess some that she imagined a year would be endless so she accepted his proposal on the spot. No sooner had she promised Ricky with the Tuft that she would

marry him that same day in one year's time than she felt a great change come over her. From that moment, she began such a brilliant and witty conversation with Ricky that he thought he must have given her more intelligence than he had kept for himself.

When she went home to the palace, the courtiers did not know what to think of the sudden and extraordinary change in her. Before, she had babbled idiocies; now she said the wisest things, and always with a sweet touch of wit. Everyone was overjoyed, except her younger sister whose nose was put sadly out of joint because, now she no longer outshone her sister in conversation, nothing detracted from her ugliness and she looked the plain little thing she really was beside her.

The king took advice from his counsellors. The news of the change in the princess was publicly announced and all the young princes from the neighbouring kingdoms tried to make her fall in love with them. But she found that not one of them was half as clever as she was and she listened to all their protestations unmoved. However, at last there came a prince so powerful, so rich and so handsome that she felt her interest quicken slightly. Her father told her that she could choose her own husband from among her suitors. She thanked him and asked him for a little time in which to decide.

So that she could make up her mind in peace she went off for a walk by herself and, by chance, she found herself in the same wood where she had met Ricky with the Tuft. As she walked through the wood, deep in thought, she heard a noise under her feet, as if a great many people were coming and going, hither and thither, in a great bustle, underground.

Listening attentively, she thought she heard a voice demand: "Bring me that roasting pan," and another say: "Fetch me the saucepan," and yet another cry: "Put a bit more wood on the fire." Then the very ground opened in front of her and she saw a huge kitchen full of cooks, scullions and all the staff required to prepare a magnificent banquet. Out of the kitchen came a band of twenty or thirty spit-turners who at once took up their positions round a long table and, chefs caps on the sides of their heads, larding needles in hand, all went busily to work, singing away.

The princess was astonished at the spectacle and asked them who was their master.

"Why, Prince Ricky with the Tuft, madame," replied the head cook. "And tomorrow is his wedding day."

The princess was more surprised than ever. Then, in a flash, she remembered how, just a year before, she had promised to marry Ricky

with the Tuft; and when she remembered that, she thought she would faint. She had forgotten her promise completely. When she had said she would marry Ricky, she had been a fool and, as soon as she possessed all the sense the prince had given her, her earlier follies had vanished from her mind.

In a state of some agitation, she walked on but she had not gone thirty paces before Ricky with the Tuft presented himself to her, dressed like a prince on his wedding day.

"See, madame!" he said, "I have come to keep my word and I do not doubt that you are here in order to keep yours."

"I must confess to you that I have not made up my mind on that point," answered the princess, "and I fear that I do not think I shall ever be able to do as you wish."

"You astonish me, madame," said Ricky with the Tuft.

"I daresay I do," said the princess calmly. "And certainly, if I were dealing with an insensitive man, I should feel very embarrassed. An insensitive man would say to me: 'A princess must keep her word. You promised to marry me and marry me you shall.' But I know I am speaking to a subtle and perceptive man of the world and I am certain he will listen to reason. As you know, when I was a fool, I could not bring myself to a firm decision concerning our marriage. Now I have the brains you gave me, I am even more difficult to please than I was then. And would you wish me to make a decision today that I could not make when I had no sense? If you wished to marry me, you did me a great wrong to take away my stupidity and make me see clearly things I never saw before."

Ricky with the Tuft replied:

"If an insensitive man would be justified in reproaching you for breaking your word, why should you expect, madame, that I should not behave in the same way when my whole life's happiness is at stake? Is it reasonable that a sensitive man should be treated worse than an insensitive one? Would you say that, when you possess so much reason yourself, and wanted it so much? But let us come to the point. With the single exception of my ugliness, is there anything in me that displeases you? Are you dissatisfied with my birth, my intelligence, my personality or my behaviour?"

"Not at all," replied the princess. "I love everything about you except your person."

"If that is so, then I am going to be very happy," said Ricky with the Tuft. "For you alone can make me the handsomest of men."

"How can I do that?" asked the princess.

"By loving me enough to make it come true," said Ricky. "The fairy midwife who gave me the power to make the one I loved wise and witty also gave you the power to make the one you love as beautiful as you are yourself, if you truly wish it so."

"If that is the way of things," said the princess, "I wish with all my heart that you may become the handsomest prince in all the world."

As soon as she said that, Ricky with the Tuft seemed to her the handsomest man she had ever seen.

But some people say there was no magic involved in this transformation and love alone performed the miracle. They whispered that when the princess took into account her lover's faithfulness, his sense, his good qualities, and his intellect, then she no longer saw how warped his body was nor how ugly his face. His hump seemed to her no more than good, broad shoulders; at first she thought he had a frightful limp but now she saw it was really a charming, scholarly stoop. His eyes only sparkled the more because of his squint and she knew that squint was due to the violence of his passion. And how martial, how heroic, she thought his huge, red nose was!

Be that as it may, the princess promised to marry him there and then, provided he obtained the consent of the king, her father.

The king saw how much in love his daughter was with Ricky with the Tuft and, besides, he knew him for a wise and prudent prince. He accepted him as his son-in-law with pleasure.

The next day, the wedding was celebrated just as Ricky had foreseen, according to the arrangements he had made a year before.

Moral

This is not a fairy tale but the plain, unvarnished truth; every feature of the face of the one we love is beautiful, every word the beloved says is wise.

Another moral

A beautiful soul is one thing, a beautiful face another. But love alone can touch the heart.

Cinderella:

or, The Little Glass Slipper

There once lived a man who married twice, and his second wife was the haughtiest and most stuck-up woman in the world. She already had two daughters of her own and her children took after her in every way. Her new husband's first wife had given him a daughter of his own before she died, but she was a lovely and sweet-natured girl, very like her own natural mother, who had been a kind and gentle woman.

The second wedding was hardly over before the stepmother showed her true colours. Her new daughter was so lovable that she made her own children seem even more unpleasant, by contrast; so she found the girl insufferable. She gave her all the rough work about the house to do, washing the pots and pans, cleaning out Madame's bedroom and those of her step-sisters, too. She slept at the top of the house, in a garret, on a thin, lumpy mattress, while her step-sisters had rooms with fitted carpets, soft beds and mirrors in which they could see themselves from head to foot. The poor girl bore everything patiently and dared not complain to her father because he would have lost his temper with her. His new wife ruled him with a rod of iron.

When the housework was all done, she would tuck herself away in the chimney corner to sit quietly among the cinders, the only place of privacy she could find, and so the family nicknamed her Cinderbritches. But the younger sister, who was less spiteful than the older one, changed her nickname to Cinderella. Yet even in her dirty clothes, Cinderella could not help but be a hundred times more beautiful than her sisters, however magnificently they dressed themselves up.

The king's son decided to hold a ball to which he invited all the aristocracy. Our two young ladies received their invitations, for they were well connected. Busy and happy, they set about choosing the dresses and hairstyles that would suit them best and that made more work for Cinderella, who had to iron her sisters' petticoats and starch their ruffles. They could talk about nothing except what they were going to wear.

"I shall wear my red velvet with the lace trimming," said the eldest.

"Well, I shall wear just a simple skirt but put my coat with the golden flowers over it and, of course, there's always my diamond necklace, which is really rather special," said the youngest.

They sent for a good hairdresser to cut and curl their hair and they bought the best cosmetics. They called Cinderella to ask for her advice, because she had excellent taste. Cinderella helped them to look as pretty as they could and they were very glad of her assistance, although they did not show it.

As she was combing their hair, they said to her:

"Cindrella, dear, wouldn't you like to go to the ball yourself?"

"Oh, don't make fun of me, my ladies, how could I possibly go to the ball!"

"Quite right, too; everyone would laugh themselves silly to see Cinder-britches at a ball."

Any other girl but Cinderella would have made horrid tangles of their hair after that, out of spite; but she was kind, and resisted the temptation. The step-sisters could not eat for two days, they were so excited. They broke more than a dozen corset-laces because they pulled them in so tightly in order to make themselves look slender and they were always primping in front of the mirror.

At last the great day arrived. When they went off, Cinderella watched them until they were out of sight and then began to cry. Her godmother saw how she was crying and asked her what the matter was.

"I want . . . I want to . . ."

But Cinderella was crying so hard she could not get the words out.

Her godmother was a fairy. She said: "I think you're crying because you want to go to the ball."

"Yes," said Cinderella, sighing.

"If you are a good girl, I'll send you there," said her godmother.

She took her into her own room and said:

"Go into the garden and pick me a pumpkin."

Cinderella went out to the garden and picked the finest pumpkin she could find. She took it to her godmother, although she could not imagine how a pumpkin was going to help her get to the ball. Her godmother hollowed out the pumpkin until there was nothing left but the shell, struck it with her ring—and instantly the pumpkin changed into a beautiful golden coach.

Then the godmother went to look in the mousetrap, and found six live mice there. She told Cinderella to lift up the lid of the trap enough to let the mice come out one by one and, as each mouse crept out, she struck it lightly with her ring. At the touch of the ring, each mouse changed into a carriage horse. Soon the coach had six dappled greys to draw it.

Then she asked herself what would do for a coachman.

"I'll go and see if there is a rat in the rat-trap," said Cinderella. "A rat would make a splendid coachman."

"Yes, indeed," said her godmother. "Go and see."

There were three fat rats in the rat-trap that Cinderella brought to her. One had particularly fine whiskers, so the godmother chose that one; when she struck him with her ring, he changed into a plump coachman who had the most imposing moustache you could wish to see.

"If you look behind the watering-can in the garden, you'll find six lizards," the godmother told Cinderella. "Bring them to me."

No sooner had Cinderella brought them to her godmother than the lizards were all changed into footmen, who stepped up behind the carriage in their laced uniforms and hung on as if they had done nothing else all their lives.

The fairy said to Cinderella:

"There you are! Now you can go to the ball. Aren't you pleased?"

"Yes, of course. But how can I possibly go to the ball in these wretched rags?"

The godmother had only to touch her with her ring and Cinderella's workaday overalls and apron changed into a dress of cloth of gold and silver, embroidered with precious stones. Then she gave her the prettiest pair of glass slippers. Now Cinderella was ready, she climbed into the coach; but her godmother told her she must be home by midnight because if she stayed at the ball one moment more, her coach would turn back into a pumpkin, her horses to mice, her footmen to lizards and her clothes back into overalls again.

She promised her godmother that she would be sure to return from the ball before midnight. Then she drove off. The king's son had been told that a great princess, hitherto unknown to anyone present, was about to arrive at the ball and ran to receive her. He himself helped her down from her carriage with his royal hand and led her into the ballroom where all the guests were assembled. As soon as they saw her, an enormous silence descended. The dancing ceased, the fiddlers forgot to ply their bows as the entire company gazed at this unknown lady. The only sound in the entire ballroom was a confused murmur:

"Oh, isn't she beautiful!"

Even the king himself, although he was an old man, could not help gazing at her and remarked to the queen that he had not seen such a lovely young lady for a long time. All the women studied her hair and her ball-gown attentively so that they would be able to copy them the next day, provided they could find such a capable hairdresser, such a skilful dressmaker, such magnificent silk.

The king's son seated her in the most honoured place and then led her on to the dance floor; she danced so gracefully, she was still more admired. Then there was a fine supper but the prince could not eat at all, he was too preoccupied with the young lady. She herself went and sat beside her sisters and devoted herself to entertaining them. She shared the oranges and lemons the prince had given her with them and that surprised them very much, for they did not recognise her.

While they were talking, Cinderella heard the chimes of the clock striking a quarter to twelve. She made a deep curtsey and then ran off as quickly as she could. As soon as she got home, she went to find her godmother and thanked her and told her how much she wanted to go to the ball that was to be given the following day, because the king's son had begged her to. While she was telling her godmother everything that had happened, her step-sisters knocked at the door. Cinderella hurried to let them in.

"What a long time you've been!" she said to them yawning, rubbing her eyes and stretching as if she could scarcely keep awake, although she had not wanted to sleep for a single moment since they had left the house.

"If you had come to the ball, you wouldn't have been sleepy!" said one of the sisters. "The most beautiful princess you ever saw arrived unexpectedly and she was so kind to us, she gave us oranges and lemons."

Cinderella asked the name of the princess but they told her nobody knew it, and the king's son was in great distress and would give anything to find out more about her. Cinderella smiled and said:

"Was she really so very beautiful? Goodness me, how lucky you are. And can I never see her for myself? What a shame! Miss Javotte, lend me that old yellow dress you wear around the house so that I can go to the ball tomorrow and see her for myself."

"What?" exclaimed Javotte. "Lend my dress to such a grubby little Cinderbritches as it is—it must think I've lost my reason!"

Cinderella had expected a refusal; and she would have been exceedingly embarrassed if her sister had relented and agreed to lend her a dress and taken her to the ball in it.

Next day, the sisters went off to the ball again. Cinderella went, too, but this time she was even more beautifully dressed than the first time. The king's son did not leave her side and never stopped paying her compliments so that the young girl was utterly absorbed in him and time passed so quickly that she thought it must still be only eleven o'clock when she heard the chimes of midnight. She sprang to her feet and darted off as lightly as a doe. The prince sprang after her but he could not catch her; in her flight, however, she let fall one of her glass slippers and the prince tenderly picked it up. Cinderella arrived home out of breath, without her carriage, without her footmen, in her dirty old clothes again; nothing remained of all her splendour but one of her little slippers, the pair of the one she had dropped. The prince asked the guards at the palace gate if they had seen a princess go out; they replied they had seen nobody leave the castle last night at midnight but a ragged young girl who looked more like a kitchen-maid than a fine lady.

When her sisters came home from the ball, Cinderella asked them if they had enjoyed themselves again; and had the beautiful princess been there? They said, yes; but she had fled at the very stroke of midnight, and so promptly that she had dropped one of her little glass slippers. The king's son had found it and never took his eyes off it for the rest of the evening, so plainly he was very much in love with the beautiful lady to whom it belonged.

They spoke the truth. A few days later, the king's son publicly announced that he would marry whoever possessed the foot for which the glass slipper had been made. They made a start by trying the slipper on the feet of all the princesses; then moved on to the duchesses, then to the rest of the court, but all in vain. At last they brought the slipper to the two sisters, who did all they could to squeeze their feet into the slipper but could not manage it, no matter how hard they tried. Cinderella watched them; she recognised her own slipper at once. She laughed, and said:

"I'd like to try and see if it might not fit me!"

Her sisters giggled and made fun of her but the gentleman who was in charge of the slipper trial looked at Cinderella carefully and saw how beautiful she was. Yes, he said; of course she could try on the slipper. He had received orders to try the slipper on the feet of every girl in the

kingdom. He sat Cinderella down and, as soon as he saw her foot, he knew it would fit the slipper perfectly. The two sisters were very much astonished but not half so astonished as they were when Cinderella took her own glass slipper from her pocket. At that the godmother appeared; she struck Cinderella's overalls with her ring and at once the old clothes were transformed to garments more magnificent than all her ball-dresses.

Then her sisters knew she had been the beautiful lady they had seen at the ball. They threw themselves at her feet to beg her to forgive them for all the bad treatment she had received from them. Cinderella raised them up and kissed them and said she forgave them with all her heart and wanted them only always to love her. Then, dressed in splendour, she was taken to the prince. He thought she was more beautiful than ever and married her a few days later. Cinderella, who was as good as she was beautiful, took her sisters to live in the palace and arranged for both of them to be married, on the same day, to great lords.

Moral

Beauty is a fine thing in a woman; it will always be admired. But charm is beyond price and worth more, in the long run. When her godmother dressed Cinderella up and told her how to behave at the ball, she instructed her in charm. Lovely ladies, this gift is worth more than a fancy hairdo; to win a heart, to reach a happy ending, charm is the true gift of the fairies. Without it, one can achieve nothing; with it, everything.

Another moral

It is certainly a great advantage to be intelligent, brave, well-born, sensible and have other similar talents given only by heaven. But however great may be your god-given store, they will never help you to get on in the world unless you have either a godfather or a godmother to put them to work for you.

Sweetheart

Once a good king went out hunting. A little rabbit jumped up into his arms to escape from the hounds. "You've come to me for help," said the king to the rabbit, petting it. "I'll take care of you." He took the rabbit back to his palace and gave it a pretty little hutch and a good meal of fresh grass.

That night, when the king was all alone, a beautiful lady appeared before him. She did not wear cloth of gold or silver but a plain dress white as snow, and no crown or tiara on her head, only a garland of white roses. The king was very surprised to see her because the door was locked and he could not imagine how she got in.

"I am the Fairy Candida," she said. "I was out walking in the wood when your hunt came by and I decided I would find out if the good things they say about you are true. So I changed into a rabbit and threw myself on your mercy, because I know that people who are kind to animals are kinder still to men and women. If you had refused to help me, I should have known you were cruel. Thank you for looking after me. Ask me for your heart's desire and I will grant it."

"I have only one son, whom I love so much I call him Sweetheart," said the king. "If you wish me well, then be a good friend to my child."

"With all my heart," said the fairy. "Your son shall be the handsomest prince in the world, or the richest, or the most powerful—only choose which you want."

"I don't want any of those things for my boy," said the king. "But I should be very much obliged to you if you were to help him to be good. For what use would good looks, wealth or power be to him if he were a wicked man? You know as well as I do that then he would be unhappy. Only the good are happy."

"Quite right," said Candida. "But it lies beyond my power to turn your Sweetheart into a good man in spite of himself. He must work hard at good deeds. I can promise you only this—I shall give him sound advice, point out his faults to him, and, if he shows no sign of mending his ways, then I shall punish him."

The fairy's promise made the king very happy and he died soon afterwards. Two days after the old king died, the Fairy Candida appeared to Sweetheart.

"I promised your father that I would be your friend," she said. "I have come to keep my word. Here is a present."

She slipped a plain little gold ring on Sweetheart's finger.

"Look after this ring; it is more precious than diamonds. Each time you commit a bad deed, the ring will prick your finger, and, if you go on doing bad deeds, in spite of the pricking, then you will no longer be a friend of mine and I shall turn against you."

The fairy vanished. Sweetheart was very startled and, after that, for a long time, he behaved so well that the ring never pricked him once. But, one day, out hunting, the animals all refused to be caught and that put him in a bad temper. He felt the ring give his finger a little squeeze, but it did not hurt him so he did not pay it any attention.

When he got home, his pet dog came bounding up for some fun and he snapped: "Away with you! I'm not in the mood for games!" The poor little thing did not understand, of course, and went on tugging at his sleeve. Sweetheart gave the little dog a big kick and the ring pricked his finger just as if it had been a pin. The prince was so ashamed he went away and hid himself in his room.

But, after a while, he began to feel irritated. "I think that fairy is making a fool of me," he said to himself. "What did I do wrong? I only kicked a

dog that was annoying me. What point is there in being a king, if I'm not allowed to kick my own dog?"

"I had no intention of making a fool of you!" said a voice as if in reply to Sweetheart's secret thoughts. "And now you've made everything much worse. You lost your temper because you can't bear to be crossed, even in sport. That is bad enough. Then you kicked a little dog who had done nothing wrong. I know you are bigger and more important than a dog, but that is no excuse for bullying. Being a king does *not* mean you can do exactly as you please. It means you must do as well as you can, every minute of the day."

Sweetheart knew he was in the wrong and promised to do better in future, but he did not keep his word. The old nurse who looked after him when he was a baby had thoroughly spoiled him. If he wanted anything, he need only cry, or sulk, or stamp his foot, and he got it. Morning, noon and night, the old nurse told him how one day he would be a king and kings were happy because everybody jumped when they said, "jump". Sweetheart grew up and started to think for himself and then he saw how unlovable his selfish ways were. He tried and tried to be good, but bad habits are hard to break, although he was not naturally bad-hearted, only used to getting his own way in everything.

He often cried when he gave in to his worse self but he never blamed himself for what he did; he felt sorry for himself and said: "If only they had been stricter with me when I was little, I would not suffer so much today!"

The ring pricked him all the time. Because it pricked him only a little bit for peccadilloes, sometimes he ignored it and went on with whatever mild meanness he was doing. But, when he was really bad, then the ring drew blood and that would stop him in his tracks.

At last he could bear it no longer. He wanted to be wicked in comfort so much that he took off the ring and threw it away. How happy he was to be rid of those sore fingers! He threw himself into bad deeds with a will and soon became insufferable.

One day, in the street, Sweetheart saw such a beautiful girl he decided, on the spot, to marry her. She was called Zélie and was not only beautiful but wise. Sweetheart thought she would be happy to become queen, but Zélie said: "Although I am only a penniless shepherdess, I can never marry you, sir."

"Don't you think I'm attractive?" said Sweetheart, put out.

"Handsome is as handsome does," said Zélie. "What good would your handsome face be to me, or your money, or the fine clothes and carriages you would buy me, if, day in, day out, you made me despise you by the way you carried on?"

When Sweetheart heard that, he was so angry with Zélie that he ordered his guards to arrest her and lock her up in a room in his palace. He brooded and brooded over the contemptuous way the girl had spoken but he still loved her, and even he could not quite bring himself to punish her for speaking her mind.

Sweetheart's old nurse had a son of her own and this man made it his business to carry on the family tradition of flattering, pampering and spoiling the prince. When he saw that Sweetheart was downcast, he wanted to know why. He laughed when he heard Sweetheart had reluctantly decided to mend his ways so that the shepherdess would start to love him.

"Well, well, well!" said the bad friend. "Why on earth do you let that insignificant little miss order you around? If I were in your shoes, she would do what I wanted, or else! Remember you are a king, and she is only a shepherdess, with whims. Put her in your deepest dungeon on a diet of bread and water. If she still refuses to marry you, why, do away with her—to teach the rest a lesson! You must let your subjects know they were born to do your bidding and that alone."

"But Zélie hasn't done anything wrong," said Sweetheart.

"Yes, she has," said the bad friend. "She has disobeyed you."

So Sweetheart was persuaded. He was so scared that the people of his kingdom would make fun of him for behaving like a human being instead of a king that he did not listen to the voices inside him that told him he was doing wrong. At supper he drank a good deal of wine to give him courage, and then went off to Zélie to tell her that either she must marry him, or—

But, when Sweetheart burst through her door, Zélie was gone.

His wrath was terrible to behold. He swore vengeance on anyone who had helped Zélie to escape. Sweetheart's bad friend knew that only one man stood in the way of his influence over the prince, and that was the old tutor, who loved him. The honest old man often let Sweetheart know what he thought of him and, at first, Sweetheart used to thank him, but soon he grew impatient with him because his tutor seemed to do nothing but find fault with him although his bad friend told him all the time that he had no faults at all. Now the bad friend told Sweetheart the old tutor had plotted Zélie's rescue and Sweetheart reached new heights of fury. He ordered the guards to chain his tutor up, like a criminal.

Then Sweetheart swept off to his room in a huff, but no sooner had he slammed the door than the Fairy Candida arrived in a clap of thunder and she looked exceedingly stern.

"I promised your father to give you good advice and to punish you if you did not take it," she said. "You have taken no notice of me. And now you have nothing left about you of humanity but the mere appearance of a man. You have become a perfect monster. Henceforward, you shall look like what you are—angry as a lion, brutal as a bull, greedy as a wolf, and treacherous as a snake—why, you even wanted to destroy the loving tutor who was a second father to you! Take on in your new shape something beastly from all these creatures."

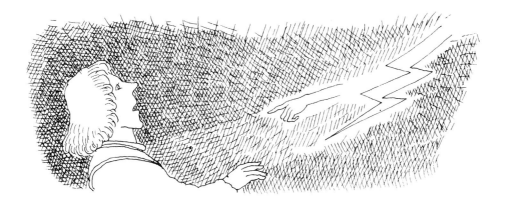

Sweetheart was whisked up and away from his palace, and dropped down in the middle of a trackless forest, beside a clear pool, in which, to his horror, he saw the reflection of his new self—head of a lion, with a bull's horns on top; limbs of a wolf; and a long, snaky tail.

An unseen voice said gravely: "See to what a state your bad deeds have brought you! And yet your soul is still more ugly than your body!"

Sweetheart knew the voice belonged to the Fairy Candida and raged round the pool, seeking her so that he could devour her, but she remained invisible although he could hear her laughing.

"You really do look very comic, in such a tizzy! And now I'm going to bring down your pride, Sweetheart. I shall put you, helpless, in the hands of the people of your own kingdom."

Sweetheart ran away from the mirror of the pool, so that he could not see his own ugly shape any more, but, before he went far, he tumbled into a pit and lay there.

Trappers had dug this pit in order to catch bears and now they caught Sweetheart. They tied him up and took him off to town. Not for one moment did Sweetheart pause in his raging and think: "All this is my fault!" Far from it! All the way to town, he roundly cursed the Fairy Candida, bit at his bonds and roared. When they drew near the town, they saw the signs of great rejoicing because everyone thought a thunderbolt had come down from heaven and blown away wicked Sweetheart, the worst king in the world. And good riddance.

But that was not all that had taken place since the Fairy Candida took charge of Sweetheart. His bad friend thought he would like to be king himself, once Sweetheart was gone, but the people rose up against him and tore him to pieces, and then offered the crown to Sweetheart's own wise old tutor.

"Today is coronation day," the townspeople told the bear-trappers. "And we are all very pleased."

Sweetheart hissed and sputtered with fury when he heard that but he felt much worse when they arrived at the square in front of the palace, for there sat his tutor, on a throne, and the entire kingdom, gathered together, all cried: "Long live the king!" Because the new king would need to live a long time in order to put right the harm that Sweetheart had done.

Then the new king raised his hand for silence and said: "I accept the crown you offer me but I do so in order to keep it in trust for Prince

Sweetheart. A fairy revealed to me that he is not dead and, perhaps, one day he will come back to us, just as he was when he was a boy, when his father was alive, and he was full of promise, before flattery turned his head. And then all his inheritance will be returned to him."

Those words of his old tutor's went straight to Sweetheart's heart. He realised how much the old man loved him. For the first time, he reproached himself for his crimes and, as he did so, the rage that consumed him died down. He remembered his past, and told himself that his punishment was far less than he deserved. He stopped clawing furiously at the bars of his cage and lay down, all at once as gentle as a lamb. He was taken to a menagerie where wild beasts were kept, and left there.

The keeper was a cruel man who often beat him when he was in the mood. One day, as the keeper was taking a nap, a tiger broke its leash and jumped on the sleeping keeper. Sweetheart was glad to see the keeper about to get his just desserts until he thought: "No! I must return good for evil. I shall save that cruel man's life."

At that, the bars of his cage parted and Sweetheart sprang out. The keeper woke up and fought for his life. He thought his end had come when

the peculiar-looking monster broke free and pitched into the battle but, when Sweetheart overcame the tiger, he lay down peacefully at the feet of the man he had rescued and purred. The grateful keeper bent down to embrace the monster but an invisible voice announced: "One good deed deserves another," and then, instead of a monster, on the ground there lay a pretty little dog.

Sweetheart was delighted to be a dog instead of a monster. The keeper picked him up and took him to the new queen. She made a great pet of him and it would have been a fine life for a dog, but Sweetheart was not really a dog, he was a man, inside. All the same, he made the best of it, although his mistress decided her puppy was growing up too quickly and put him on a strict diet—bread, nothing but bread, and not much of that! So Sweetheart was always hungry, but he bore it with patience.

One day, he decided to make a picnic of his half a loaf, and trotted off with the bread in his mouth through the palace gardens towards a favourite little stream. But, lo and behold! the stream had vanished and, in its place, stood a shining house made of gold and precious stones. All kinds of men and women in lovely clothes were hurrying eagerly inside to join in the merry-making that went on there, but those who came out of the house were pale, thin and covered with sores, and their clothes were in rags. Some fell down because they could walk no further, others dragged themselves along on their hands and knees. Still others lay on the ground and begged for crusts, but nobody fed them. One beggar girl began to pull up grass and eat it. Sweetheart said to himself: "I am very hungry, but I certainly won't starve to death before dinnertime. If I give this girl my lunch, it might save her life."

So he gave the girl his crust. As soon as she ate it, she started to smile. Sweetheart, content, turned to go home, but he saw four big guardsmen

dragging Zélie towards the house. Then Sweetheart was sorry he was no longer a monster, because when he was big and fierce, then he could easily have saved her but, now he was a little dog, all he could do was run beside them, snapping and barking. The guards kicked him away and locked Zélie up inside the house. Sweetheart remembered how he himself had once locked her up and was filled with remorse.

As he crouched under her window, it flew open, and there was Zélie, throwing out a plateful of what looked like the most delicious food. He had eaten nothing all day and thought that perhaps these good things were a reward. Just as he was about to tuck in, the beggar girl to whom he had given his bread snatched him up in her arms.

"Don't eat!" she said. "This magic house is called, the Mansion of Greed, and everything that comes out of it is poisoned."

And a mysterious voice said: "So you see, again, how one good deed provokes another!"

At that, Sweetheart found he was no longer a puppy but had turned into a dove, with plumage as white as the dress of the Fairy Candida. When he saw how white he had become, he dared hope the fairy was beginning to forgive him. But, first, he must find Zélie.

He flew into the Mansion of Greed and fluttered through every room, but she was no longer there. He flew out to search the whole, wide world. He flew day and night, night and day, until, crossing the desert, he saw her, at last, seated at the mouth of a cave sharing a frugal supper with an old holy man. Sweetheart joyfully settled on her shoulder, cooing and pecking softly at her cheek to show how pleased he was to see her. Zélie laughed and stroked his feathers with her hand.

"See how he wants to be my bird!" she said. "Dear little dove, I will always love you."

"What have you said, Zélie?" cried the hermit. "What have you promised?"

Then Sweetheart turned back into his own natural self.

"Yes, Zélie," he said. "When you said that you would always love me, I became myself, again. Tell me you will marry me, or else I must beg my fairy godmother to change me into whatever shape would please you better than this one."

His fairy godmother, the Fairy Candida, threw off her holy man's disguise and said: "Don't be afraid. Zélie won't change her mind. She fell

in love with you the first time she saw you, but how could a girl of such character marry the rogue you were, then? Now you have learned your lesson and are a changed man. She can love you without reservations. Go home and live happily ever after."

Immediately they found themselves back in Sweetheart's own palace, standing in front of his good old tutor, who was delighted to see his repentant prince returned again, and gave him back his kingdom on the spot. Sweetheart and Zélie ruled together in harmony, and, although now he kept the magic ring on his finger all the time, never again did he give it cause to prick him.

About the Stories

The stories in this book were all written down for the first time in French, in the seventeenth and eighteenth centuries, during the time there was coming about that general discovery of the special nature of childhood whose origins are discussed in Philippe Ariès' book, *Centuries of Childhood*. The idea that children might be different not only in stature but also in nature to adults had a profound effect on European society as it slowly spread. By the mid-eighteenth century, under the influence of the philosophy of Jean-Jacques Rousseau, the nurturing of children had become a subject of profound intellectual debate as childhood itself, no longer seen as a brief prologue to grown-up life, started to last longer. Now childhood required clothes of its own, not baby clothes nor cut-down grown-up clothes; it also needed books of its own.

The production of books specifically intended to edify children expanded rapidly in Europe during this period, although the idea of what constituted such edification changed, too. For Perrault, in the late seventeenth century, children are still apprentice adults who will benefit from advice on how to charm, whom to trust, how to grow rich; his fairy tales are parables of instruction. Madame Leprince de Beaumont, young enough to have been his granddaughter, believes that children need only be *good* in order to deserve happy endings.

However, when Charles Perrault first wrote down the fairy tales that have come to us under his name, they had already existed, in various forms, for centuries, part of the unwritten tradition of folk-lore handed down by word of mouth. Nor do his stories belong exclusively to France; folk-lore acknowledges no frontiers. And, if Madame de Beaumont, writing rather later, shapes her tales with more glamour and less fidelity to source material, her *Beauty and the Beast* still has its origins deep in the antique, international heritage of the folk-tale. Similar "beast marriage" stories in which girls marry goats, monkeys, bears, crocodiles, occur all over the world. These writers, among the first self-conscious writers for children, wisely chose to offer children either the very same stories, or tales in the style of those stories, that had already satisfied generations with marvels of unfortunate princesses and magical transformations.

The difference was, these stories were printed in books for children themselves to read. They had been taken out of the mouths of grannies, nannies and old wives, skilfully retold, and, once in print, became "fixed" in forms that have remained remarkably unaltered until our own day, even when they have reverted again to the oral tradition. (My own grandmother, a mono-glot Yorkshirewoman, told me *Red Riding Hood* in almost Perrault's own words, forty years ago.) The formal perfection, tenderness and wit with which Madame de Beaumont retold *Beauty and the Beast* remain impossible to improve upon.

Charles Perrault was born in 1628 and died in 1703; Madame de Beaumont lived from 1711 to 1780. The difference in their method of story-telling tells us a little about the changing history of taste over the century and a half they, together, span. Perrault, a barrister's son, struck a blow for the emancipation of children early; at nine years old, enrolled in the Collège de Beauvais, he quarrelled so badly with his philosophy teacher that he emancipated himself from formal schooling. This did him no harm. He became a civil servant, scribbling verses in his spare time; eventually employed as secretary to the great statesman, Jean Baptiste Colbert, he selected the architects that designed Versailles and the Louvre. He was a self-consciously pro-gressive man, who became a rich and powerful bourgeoise apt to believe, perhaps, that no happy ending comes without the enlightened self-interest with which he credits Puss in Boots.

He married a young wife, late, in 1671. Before she died in 1678, she bore three children, in whom Perrault took a still-unfashionable de-light. His youngest son, Pierre, even has his name

as author on the first edition of a little book of fairy tales, *Histoires et Contes de Temps Passé avec des Moralités*, of 1697. Whether young Pierre had a hand in the composition or not is now beyond surmise, although the boy would have been nineteen, too old for fairy tales, when it first appeared. Perhaps a child first drew an indulgent father's attention to the stories of a country-bred nursemaid. The elder Perrault, a member of the Académie Française, had already shown an interest in fairy tales; he had published versions of *The Foolish Wishes* and *Donkey-Skin*, both translated here. And it was a sophisti-cated hand that polished and rationalised the old stories, adding the moral tags that temper their darkness and magic with good-natured cynic-ism. This hand firmly puts the bloodthirsty antics of Bluebeard in the barbaric past: no modern husband, says the moral, would dare behave like that! The brutality of the traditional tale offers the opportunity for good advice; if the wolf *does* eat Red Riding Hood, says Perrault briskly, what else can you expect if you talk to strangers?

Histoires et Contes de Temps Passé avec des Moralités contains what have become the stan-dard versions of most of what are now the classic fairy tales: *Sleeping Beauty, Little Red Riding Hood, Bluebeard, Cinderella, Hop o' My Thumb, Puss in Boots, Diamonds and Toads* (called here, as Perrault calls it, *The Fairies*), and *Ricky with the Tuft*. As *Mother Goose Tales*, they arrived in English in 1729 and went directly into that common heritage presided over by the mythical old lady of that name with the inex-haustible fund of stories and rhymes, whose sometimes cruel and grotesque imagination has been tempered by the civilised Parisian gentle-man who saw the irony in most things, even in cannibal mothers-in-law and ravening wolves. And whose fairies, the Lilac Fairy, Cinderella's godmother and the rest, have less the air of supernatural beings than of worldly, influential patrons, such as Colbert was to him.

Each century tends to re-create fairy tales after its own fashion. If Perrault's work helped initiate

a vogue for fairy tales at the court of Louis XIV, the fairy tale developed a rococo magnificence alien to Perrault's salty rationality but quite in keeping with the boundless extravagance that characterised the French court of the time.

Now the fairy tale lost all contact with the illiterate peasantry and, indeed, with children. It became a highly developed literary form composed by genteel hobbyists who presumed a leisured, adult audience with a taste for high-flown whimsy. The fashion continued through out the eighteenth century; an anthology of fairy tales in forty-one volumes, *Le Cabinet des Fées*, edited by Charles-Joseph de Mayer, appeared as late as 1789. The fashion terminated abruptly with the French Revolution.

Madame Leprince de Beaumont, however, worked exclusively for young people, both as a writer and a governess. Her talent for the "literary" fairy tale combined with an enthusiasm for education. She herself was a person who could not have existed before her own time; a respected and respectable woman who earned her own living. Her very existence, and her contemporary fame, is symptomatic of social change.

Her *Magasin des enfants, ou dialogues entre une sage Gouvernante et plusieurs de ses Élèves*, was printed in London in 1756. The book intended to blend "the useful" with "the agreeable" in the form of a collection of moral tales, of which *Beauty and the Beast* is one. It was translated as *The Young Misses Magazine* in 1761. Although Madame de Beaumont derived the structure of *Beauty and the Beast*, from another woman writer, Madame Gabrielle Susanne Barbot de Gallon de Villeneuve, Madame de Beaumont exercises a miracle of compression on her source, which runs to 362 pages in Madame de Villeneuve's *Les Contes Marins* of 1740.

Madame de Beaumont's *Beauty and the Beast* is not only the "classic text", as Iona and Peter Opie put it, "of the world-wide beast-marriage story", but one of the finest, as it is one of the earliest, of all short stories. Whilst retaining the mood and the motifs of the fairy tale, she has moved well beyond the scope or the intention of

Perrault. There is real inner life to her characters and Beauty, with her stoicism, courage and kindness, is a fully-realised heroine in the manner of modern fiction rather than in the two-dimensional mode of the fairy tale. Her relationship with her father has a complex sensitivity you will not find in, say, *Cinderella*, where Cinderella's father is no more than a function of the plot. Madame de Beaumont infuses her narrative with a subjectivity of feeling which is worlds away from the matter-of-fact narrative of Perrault and his sources.

Not for Madame de Beaumont the bright colours, precise outlines and stock adjectives of Perrault's radiant simplicity, which is still akin to the old wives' country story telling; her prose is self-conscious, sensuous, evocative. With Beauty's father, we shiver in the cold wind in the wood, shudder to hear the Beast's frightful roar; the haunted solitude of the Beast's palace enchants us as it does Beauty. We live inside the story until we, too, like Beauty, are almost sad to find, when we have learned to love the dear, ugly, irreplaceable Beast, that, after all, he is no more than a common or garden enchanted prince. (Ricky with the Tuft, however, remains just as ugly as he ever was when his princess starts to love him; all that has changed is how the princess sees him, for, as Perrault's moral points out, "every feature of the one we love is beautiful". An increase in the subtlety of the expression of emotion does not necessarily mean an in-

creased subtlety in the quality of that emotion.)

The exquisite music of Madame de Beaumont's prose, the ineradicable sense of melancholy that pervades the story in spite of, almost because of, the happy ending, the somewhat over-determined moralising (even more evident in her *Sweetheart*, here translated, too), indicate how the Age of Reason is giving way to the Cult of Sensibility, of which moral exhortation is a part. The subjectivity of her manner of telling is part of the beauty of the tale and the whole of the moral, which is all to do with something indefinable, not with "doing well", but with "being good". Beauty's happiness is founded on her abstract quality of virtue; Prince Sweetheart can only be happy if he is good and is saved by the love of a good woman. Seventy or eighty years before the "sage gouvernante" discussed virtue with her pupils in a manner, perhaps, not unlike that of the Fairy Candida in *Prince Sweetheart*—that is, "being good" is "doing what you're told"—Perrault added an ad hoc collection of morals to his tales, from which his readers could choose the one they liked best. He applauded the ingenity of a quick-witted con man like Puss in Boots. The boy who ran away from school admired inventiveness. Madame de Beaumont is not like that.

In her lovely stories, we see the fairy tale melting into both a magical art, and also into the kind of abstract moralising that would dominate nineteenth century stories for children.

128